Pumpkin Spice Secrets

Pumpkin Spice Secrets

Hillary Homzie

SCHOLASTIC INC.

This is a work of fiction. Names, characters, places, and incidents are from the author's imagination, and used fictitiously.

ISBN 978-1-338-32534-8

12 11 10 9 8 7 6 5 4 3 2 1 18 19 20 21 22 23

Printed in the U.S.A. 40

First Scholastic printing, October 2018

Cover design by Liz Casal
Cover photo credit iStock

Chapter One:
Sweet Meet

"Order anything you want," says my sister, Elvie. We're at the Friendly Bean Café in the shopping center close to our house. The whole place smells like coffee, whipped cream, and chocolate.

"Anything?" I ask. When Mom takes me here she only lets me get hot cocoa. She still thinks I'm five.

Elvie smiles. "Anything. It's my treat."

Okay, right now I'm thinking—big sisters are awesome. Three people stand in line in front of us. It's Saturday afternoon and the place is packed. At the tables, moms chat together while their toddlers happily munch on cookies. High school kids gossip and laugh, and some customers sit by themselves looking at their phones or reading the newspaper. There's a hissing sound as the barista steams milk behind the counter.

Elvie drove me to the Friendly Bean to talk about something. I have no idea what, though. I feel excited and nervous at the same time.

"So, you promise what you want to talk about isn't anything bad?" I whisper.

Elvie shakes her head. "No, Maddie. I promise. But it is *really* important. A sister talk." She points to the menu. "Now, focus. They have frappés, cappuccinos, lattés, teas, and every kind of cookie and brownie you can imagine."

"Dessert too?" I ask as the barista knocks a small silver pitcher of frothy milk against the counter.

"Go for it!" Elvie jiggles the car keys in her hand before stuffing them into her purse. "After all, you're starting seventh grade this week."

"And you're going to be a junior," I add.

"Ugh. Don't remind me." Elvie constantly goes on about how hard her year is going to be. She's signed up for three AP courses and has been stressing about it. But I don't know why. She always gets A's.

"Okay, I promise never to bring up that being a

junior is crazy hard—except for right now." We laugh, and move up a little closer to the counter. At a nearby table, there's a group of girls whom I don't know, whispering their secrets. Somehow, even though I don't know them, they make me feel left out. Suddenly, I'm really missing my best friend, Jana Patel. She's been away with her family for two weeks up at their cabin in the White Mountains in New Hampshire. Which is about three hours from Northborough, where we live in Massachusetts.

"Why don't you tell me what you want and then grab us a seat?" says Elvie, looking behind her as more people walk through the door. "This place is getting super crowded."

I study the specials on the blackboard right next to a HELP WANTED sign. The one with the smiling jack-o'-lantern catches my eye. The drawing is really good. Plus, I love pumpkin spice. After ordering an iced pumpkin spice frappé and a pumpkin spice muffin, I put my windbreaker on the back of a chair and gaze out the window. Mom had insisted I bring it, even though it's broiling hot outside. The sun is shining brightly, and the sky is a perfect blue with frothy white clouds.

Elvie grabs our drinks, and I rush over to get mine from her.

"Here you go," she says, handing me my pumpkin spice frappé. "Your muffin is coming." She pivots around to pay at the counter. Heading back to our seats, I see two women, clutching shopping bags, about to sit down at our table. The table where I just put my windbreaker! How could they not see it?

With my frappé in my hand, I race to our table to intercept the women before they sit down.

And then somehow I don't see the boy walking in front of me to stand at the back of the line.

And then somehow I slam my plastic cup right up against him.

And then somehow the lid flips off my iced pumpkin spice frappé and it all spills onto his shirt. I mean *all* of it. The whipped cream, the caramel swirls, the sprinkles, and the icy rest of it.

The boy jerks back and lets out a groan of surprise. His voice is surprisingly deep.

"Uh oh! Spill!" cries somebody. Chairs scrape against the floor. I can feel eyes on me.

"Sorry. Sorry. Sorry," I say, at first not looking up.

And then I do. And I wish that I hadn't because the

boy looking at me is cute. Really cute. Like if he were a yearbook picture, I would stare at it all day. His eyes are sky blue. His teeth are whipped-cream white. He's got a swirl of curly reddish-brown hair on his forehead that's shaggy but still not messy, almost windblown or something. He's got these adorable dimples and his eyes look extra alive somehow. Freckles dust his nose.

I think I'm saying something like, "I'll get. Napkin. Now." But I'm not really sure.

"It's fine, seriously," says the boy. A staff person comes over and hands him a rag, and says she'll be back with a mop.

"I actually need to cool off," says the boy, waving his hand in front of his face like a fan. "Just got back from practice. It was really hot."

He's just too cute. I worry that he might be a mirage or a figment of my imagination. That I might have inhaled too much sugar. But of course I really haven't had any of my frappé yet, since it's dripping off this boy.

But I do know that I'm scrambling for the napkins. There's a stack of brown ones on a service counter to the left. They're in my fist and I almost embarrass myself further by starting to wipe the pumpkin-colored swirly sludge off his shirt, but I stop myself in time.

I try not to show any sign of distress, even though I feel so stupid right now. *Breathe*, I tell myself. *Breathe*. Among my friends I'm the calm one. The reasonable one. The one you can talk to and who won't blab.

My sister rushes over with another stack of napkins to help clean up the mess. "Sorry about that," she says to the boy, like I'm some little kid she's babysitting. "Looks like the mop person got lost." Then Elvie tells me she's going to get me a new pumpkin spice frappé and stake out a new table. After I thank her a million times, she leaves, but not before grumbling how they obviously do need more help around the place.

"If I had to clean up," says the boy, once my sister is out of sight, "I know I'd conveniently get lost too." His eyes twinkle. "It's so much work. Especially when it's a big mess."

"Yeah, well, my sister did order me the jumbo size." I can feel my face redden. His shirt is so sopped. And this time I notice it says *Northborough Middle School*. That's where I go! But I've never seen this boy before. Believe me, I would remember those eyes! Not that I'm one of the boy-crazy girls. Because I'm not. I'm just regular, I guess. You know, a couple of minor crushes last year that were really no big deal. Total opposite from Jana, who has a different crush every week and lets everyone know about it.

I want to ask this boy how he could possibly be wearing a Northborough shirt, but I'm too embarrassed. I hand him the napkins.

"Thanks," he says. "Now my shirt will smell like Thanksgiving and—" he examines what's left of the orange-y beverage in my cup.

"It's my favorite drink," I say. Okay, I've never had it before but I'm sure if I had taken a sip, it would have been my favorite drink. "I really got it everywhere!" I tap my own chest. "You still have some sprinkles on your shirt."

"Thanks," he says, as another café employee, a ponytailed guy with thick black glasses and tattoos up and down his arms, hurries over and cleans the floor with a mop.

"I guess I should buy you a new shirt or something," I say.

"I can toss it in the wash." The boy grins a lopsided

grin, and I think I'm going to melt faster than an iced coffee left outside on the broiling hot sidewalk.

I smile back at him and for a moment just stand there sort of awkwardly.

"I'm Jacob, by the way."

"Maddie." I once again study his shirt and get brave. "So you go to Northborough Middle? I don't remember seeing you . . ." My words trail off.

"Oh, that's because I used to be invisible, but my superpowers have worn off. So that's why you can see me now."

"I was wondering." I stand there grinning, knowing he's joking. But I'm really wanting to know the truth.

Squinting, he strokes his chin. "Actually, my parents were sending me to this private school. Endicott Academy. It was a pain. A long drive and whatever. I convinced them to let me transfer to Northborough this year for seventh grade. I know a ton of kids there, from my traveling soccer team."

"That's awesome," I say. "I do club soccer too."

"Cool."

There's no way I'm going to tell him that I mostly sit on the bench. Jana is the star. "Northborough Middle is where I go too." My cheeks warm. "I guess that part was obvious. Duh."

"Yeah, well, you never can be too sure." He smiles again and his eyes do that twinkle thing. The line is growing longer. It's looping to the very back of the store.

This is almost too good to be true: he's in seventh grade, and he's my height—almost five foot seven. I usually tower over all the boys.

"Well, see you around," I say lamely.

"Soon. Since school starts on Tuesday."

"Yeah, really soon, then. And the next time I see you. I promise I won't spill pumpkin spice frappé all over you."

"Something chocolaty next time, then?" He chuckles.

"Yeah," I agree. "I can do that."

My sister is waving at me from a table across the room. She sits with her back perfectly straight as if she's a model in some photo shoot. "Maddie, c'mon."

"Guess I got to go," I say.

"Yeah. Me too. I better get in line before it snakes out the door." He glances over at Elvie, who's holding my new drink over her head as if I might get lost in a giant crowd. "Your sister looks like her arm might fall off or something if you don't get over there in five seconds."

I giggle. It's true. "Well, 'bye, Jacob."

"'Bye, Maddie." He spins on his heel and officially rejoins the back of the line.

I don't look back as I head towards our new table. I'm glad Jacob can't see me, because my hands are trembling and my heart is pounding so loudly it's like when they turn the bass all the way up at a school dance. Those eyes! I feel like I may actually lift off the ground and hover over the café for the rest of the afternoon.

Chapter Two:
Sister Talk

"So, have you been listening to a word I'm saying?" asks Elvie. She takes a bite out of her chocolate chip cookie. We've been sitting down at the Friendly Bean for five minutes now, and Jacob is still in line.

"Um, yes, you were saying that middle school, seventh grade, is when things get serious." A bald guy sitting at the table next to us clacks away at his laptop. I'm surprised Elvie didn't bring hers to get in a little extra work. "Seventh grade is when they start to pile on the homework," I say.

"Exactly." She nods, and her long black ponytail swishes. Only it's true I'm not perfectly paying attention—I'm watching Jacob. Well, the back of Jacob. And those reddish-brown curls that touch the back of his neck. He's now one away from being served at the counter.

"Sixth grade is all about the transition from elementary school to middle school," explains Elvie. She clasps her hands in front of her plate. Her nails are seashell pink, practical and pretty, just like everything about her. "And in seventh grade, they're preparing you for high school. How you do this year will totally affect *everything*. Counselors look at your middle school record to see what classes to place you in for high school. If you want to get into a good university, you have to totally step it up, Maddie."

I take a bite out of my brownie. "I did fine last year."

"Yeah, but you got a B-minus in Language Arts."

"That's because of the oral reports. Mrs. Kingston made them a big part of our grade."

"Well, you have to get over it." She blows on her cappuccino and it makes a little wave of froth.

"Okay, okay," I say. "I'll try."

A server comes by asking if we have any dishes she can take away. My sister shakes her head. Then she leans forward across the table. "Mom and Dad worry," she says. "I'm just trying to help you out."

"I'll be fine," I say. "Even though I'm not as perfect as you always are."

"I'm not so perfect," says Elvie.

"Okay. Well, Mom and Dad think so."

She stirs her drink. "You have no idea about what they say to me when you're not around, Maddie. An A-minus is not good enough. I have to get all A's. A-pluses, even. They're easier on you."

I fiddle with my napkin. Jacob is now ordering. I wonder what he's going to get? "That's because I'm not as smart as you."

"That's so not true. It's just that you're more . . . distracted," she says. "And you're really good at other things. Like art." She looks back at the hand-drawn chalkboard menu next to the HELP WANTED sign. "Like, I bet you could draw all of those little colored pumpkins and cocoa beans just as well."

"Yeah, maybe." I shrug.

"That's something I could never do. It'd just be stick figures."

Jacob grabs his drink. It looks like he's getting something chocolaty. A smoothie, maybe. The piped-in music, some happy-sounding reggae, almost makes me want to get up and dance.

Elvie notices me watching him and raises her eyebrows. "You were talking to him for a *really* long time. You didn't drop that drink on purpose, did you?"

"What? No!" My eyes follow Jacob as he goes out the door. He stops for a moment, though, and turns to wave at me. I wave back, beaming. He's followed by a fit-looking woman in a yoga top and pants. She is obviously his mother. Judging by the shopping bag she's holding, she arrived later after doing some errands. I definitely would have noticed her earlier. She's really pretty, and I can tell where Jacob gets those startlingly bright eyes. She gazes at me curiously, like she knows all about the spill. My face is probably turning cherry red right now.

"It's okay," Elvie says knowingly. "I remember those days. And he *is* cute."

"Yes," I admit. And sigh. "He really is."

Elvie stirs her cappuccino. "So another thing I wanted to talk about is friendship stuff. Sort of, the rules. It's really important this year. Seventh grade can get kind of dicey. Girl drama. That kind of thing."

"I know all about it," I say. "We call it the BFF Code."

"Perfect," Elvie says. "Like, don't talk about a cool thing your best friend isn't invited to in front of her."

I nod. One time, a girl from my ceramics class invited me to go skiing for the day in New Hampshire. She wasn't someone I even knew that well. But Jana got really jealous. She can be kind of territorial. "Remember that time Jana wouldn't speak to me when I went skiing with Baylor?" I say.

"Exactly. So just remember to be a good friend. And don't gossip. At least not too much. Always stick up for your besties if they're being dissed or bullied. And never, ever go for your friends' crushes or boyfriends." I shake my head, thinking that I would *never* do that. It just wasn't right—totally against the Code.

Elvie was still talking. "Not that you have real boyfriends in middle school. But you get the idea."

It was funny hearing Elvie lecture me on all this, since as far as I know, she's never had a boyfriend. Her only romance was with the current textbook in front of her face.

I clear my throat. "Did you ever have a crush on a guy? When you were my age?"

"Oh, sure. Of course. Not that anything happened. But, yeah. There were a couple of guys. Micah Hammond in eighth grade. All of eighth grade. He wore pink shirts sometimes. Which I thought was soooo cool. He was brave enough to wear them and nobody teased him about it. And he played the ukulele. And the violin."

"So, what happened?" I asked.

Elvie glanced at her phone as it pinged with a text message. "Oh, gosh. I have a study group meeting at the house in fifteen minutes. We've gotta go."

"A study group? Before school even starts?"

"In AP English we have an assignment during the summer. That's what happens in the *really* hard classes."

I feel a flicker of irritation. It's not like I've never been in *any* hard classes.

"And we're going to read each other's work," Elvie continues, "to make sure we got it right." She peers at our empty cups. "Your drink was good, right?"

"Yes," I say. "Thanks for taking me and for the talk."

My sister comes over and puts her arm around me. "Sorry about your drink earlier. But it didn't turn out so bad, huh? The Bean was really great about it. I thought they would charge us, but they didn't."

"I know," I say. "They're awesome. This is the best place." And it is. Because it's where I met Jacob.

Chapter Three: GOTTA SPILL

I have something to tell you, I text Jana. My fingers hover above the phone. I'm so ready to spill the details about the pumpkin-spice-Jacob incident.

I'm sitting on the couch in the den, waiting for her response. It's late afternoon, and the sun streams onto the carpet from the picture window. Jana is probably busy doing a million things. Mom calls her overscheduled, which is pretty funny because it's not like my sister and I are un-busy. Elvie does cross-country, plays the upright bass in the youth symphony, and volunteers at a childcare center. And I have club soccer, ceramics class, and piano lessons. But I'm not so sure that I'm really into any of them. I feel like I still haven't found my thing yet.

One thing is for sure, I'm tired of waiting for Jana to text me back.

Biting my lip, I resist the urge to shake my phone. I've been waiting two whole minutes.

My phone suddenly pings! I look up from my iPad, where I've been watching a puppy cam on this cute pet website. "Finally!" I shout.

Only when I look at the phone's screen, it's not a text from Jana. It's from my soccer coach, reminding everyone of the new practice schedule. I groan loudly.

"Shh," says Elvie. She's sitting at the kitchen table, doing homework for AP US History, even though school hasn't even started yet. She's reading ahead so she can be extra prepared. Our dog, Morty, sits under the table. He's a miniature labradoodle.

When will Jana answer? This is sooooooo frustrating.

I feel all jittery inside. Like I've just drunk three frappés. Normally, awesome things happen to other people. I see them posting about it *all* the time on Snappypic and Myface. I comment on other people's awesomeness and good news *all* the time. But now, today, it's me. Which is a little weird.

I'm the kind of person who doesn't ever have drama. I just listen to my friends and help them through stuff, especially Jana with her many crushes.

Nothing usually happens to me, at least in the cute boy department. But now that something has—I really, really need to talk to her! I don't want to wait to tell Jana the details at school.

My fingers brush my phone, and part of me considers texting our other besties, Torielle Jones and Katie Wakowski. The four of us have been a group since the start of middle school. Torielle is an amazing singer—she even writes her own songs—and she's a film buff. Katie is the organizer. Last year she was class vice president. And she's also a really gifted ballet dancer. Just like Jana and me, Torielle and Katie are also best friends. Sometimes I have to pinch myself because I can't believe I'm part of this foursome. They're all so talented and awesome. But I don't text either Katie or Torielle. Since sixth grade, Jana has been my very best friend. If I told Torielle and Katie first, Jana would kill me—she'd feel so betrayed. I just can't. Jana always makes sure I'm included in everything. She would never tell Torielle and Katie anything unless I was there too.

"I need help with the groceries," Mom announces as she puts away cans of chicken noodle soup in the cupboard. "There's more bags in the van." I didn't even hear her come in. Morty did, of course. He's standing in the middle of the kitchen, his tail wagging.

I don't respond. Let Elvie help for a change.

Mom's nearby in the kitchen, wearing her Dartmouth t-shirt. That's where Elvie went to a special summer school for extra-smart kids. Mom wears that shirt practically every time she goes out, just in case you didn't already know that Elvie was in their summer gifted and talented program.

"Hello! Both of you, please come now," urges Mom as she glances at the grocery bags crammed on all the counters. Wow. That was quick. I seriously don't remember her making the trips from her minivan to the kitchen. Am I losing my mind?

"One sec," I say. The light from the sun fills the room with a perfect, golden-honey yellow. It's the same color as the pumpkin spice frappé that I had. Even though it's kind of stupid, I feel like somehow Jacob is sending me a frappé message.

"I've got to read this," insists Elvie, barely moving.

My eyes flick from the TV to my tablet, and jump back to my silent phone.

"Maddie, I need help now," Mom says. There's a hard edge to her voice.

"But why do I always have to do it? Elvie always gets out of it."

Mom slams a box of granola onto the counter. "Maddie! Put away your phone. And turn off the TV!"

I instantly regret talking back to Mom. Sometimes I feel like I'm punished any time I try to say anything around here.

Elvie bends deeper over her textbook, even more focused. Mom's eyes take in the iPad on my lap. She wipes her brow, strides into the den, and glares at me. "Is that all you have been doing while I was gone?" Her voice is sharper now. Getting to that I'm-going-to-lose-it pitch.

I close my tablet and tuck my phone between my knees so I can still glance at it. "Have you been sitting on this couch the whole time?" asks Mom. "Watching TV on your phone and turning into a couch potato?" She looks at me with dagger eyes.

Then I throw up my hands. "I've been waiting for a

text from Jana. And she's not texting me back." I look over at Elvie. She knows why.

"You know Jana is in the White Mountains at their cabin," explains Mom. "The reception is really bad. They're not driving back until late Monday night. Put your phone away. You'll just have to wait until you see her at school."

"Oh," I say, "okay." I completely knew about Jana being in New Hampshire. Why I had forgotten about the spotty Wi-Fi and phone reception? Probably because I didn't want to remember. I grab two heavy bags from the back of the mini-van to make up for my grumpiness.

The first day of school on Tuesday seems a long way off. I can't wait!

Chapter Four:

The RoadBlock

Jana's mom pulls her tan minivan alongside the curb in front of our house. It's the very first day of school. I bolt out the front door and then force myself to slow down. Seventh graders don't rush, only overeager sixth graders do.

Summer is officially over, even though it doesn't feel like it. The sky is pure blue and the sun is already out. Dew sparkles on the ivy that crawls next to the pathway to the driveway. The van door automatically whirs open, and Jana, Torielle, and Katie wave to me from the back seats. We're all wearing the same kind of jeans but with different tops, since we don't want to be too match-y. It makes me happy that we all look like we belong together. When I first started eating lunch with them last year, I always worried that I'd be on the outs. It's stupid, I know. But they're all so confident, loud, and fun.

Mom races to the sidewalk and waves at me enthusiastically as if I'm going away for a month. "Have a great first day, everyone!" she calls out. Dad already left for work. He's a lawyer and leaves early to beat the traffic.

"Morning, Maddie," says Mrs. Patel as she waves goodbye to my mom.

"Hi," I say, and nod at Jana's mom. She's dressed in a crisp shirt and perfectly pressed skirt.

I give all my friends hugs.

"You girls are actually starting seventh grade," Mrs. Patel says as she turns the steering wheel sharply to the left and pulls away from the curb. "It seems like it was just yesterday you all were in elementary school going on that outdoor ed field trip to the Berkshires."

"Or in sixth grade getting lost in school," says Torielle, shaking her head. The beads in her cornrow braids clack together.

"Not me." Jana mockingly sticks out her tongue. "I knew exactly where to go."

"Because you were walking with Katie, the human map," I say.

Katie shrugs. "Just because I studied the layout to the school doesn't mean I'm a map."

"Yes, it does," we chorus.

"Well, someone has to know where to go." Laughing, Katie now sits up extra straight in her ballerina way. She and Elvie could have a posture face-off.

In the rearview mirror, I can see Mrs. Patel shaking her head. She's pretty just like Jana, only her hair is silvery black and cut into a bob. "You look nice, Maddie," she says.

"Thanks." I feel extra sparkly today, but I don't say that part out loud.

"Hey, Maddie," says Katie. "Like that top."

I smile because it's purple—Katie's favorite color. "You should, since Torielle picked it out."

Yesterday, I had taken photos of three first-day-of-school possibilities and sent them to Torielle for a vote, since she has awesome style. I finger the little fabric flowers around the neck of my shirt. "Like your jeans, Katie," I say, with a wink. Then I glance at Jana and Torielle. "And both of yours."

My friends smile, since our jeans are obviously the

same. They all have these rhinestones in the shape of butterflies on the back pockets.

Jana leans back and gives me a high five. "Great minds think alike," we both say at the same time.

"C'mon," Jana says in her team-captain voice. "Picture time!" We put our heads together, stick out our tongues and make peace signs with our fingers. Jana holds out her phone and takes the photo. I can feel our friendship being freeze-framed and displayed like one of my soccer trophies on the shelf above my bed. It feels nice to be part of the group. In elementary school, I was a one-best-friend person. And then my best friend, Lisa, moved away to Virginia after fourth grade. Let's just say that fifth grade was a very lonely year.

But seventh grade will be the opposite of lonely.

Right now the four of us dance together to the music on the radio as Mrs. Patel turns down Church Street, where a group of runners wearing reflectors jogs on the side of the road.

Katie and Jana both start laughing at something on their phones. I lean forward to see what they are looking at. "What?" I ask.

"It's this really hysterical video," says Jana. "I'll send it to you."

"Girls, put away your phones," says Mrs. Patel. With her mom look in the mirror, she reminds us all of her no-phones-out-while-in-her-car rule. She's also going on about how she wants actual conversation, and how texting in front of others is no different than whispering secrets.

Jana puts her phone in her backpack. She rolls her eyes at me.

Katie and Torielle both stuff their phones in their pockets, and so do I.

Mrs. Patel is strict. At school, you can't have your phones out either. Unless it's during lunch.

"Maddie, I'll send you the video later," promises Jana.

"Um, okay," I lower my voice. "I can't wait till lunch!"

"Something's up," says Jana knowingly. "You want to tell us something, Maddie. You have a very mysterious smile."

"Yeah, well . . ." I trail off, thinking about Jacob.

"Tell us," urges Torielle.

Katie scoots closer. "Yes!"

"Later," I whisper, nodding significantly over at Mrs. Patel.

"Did something bad happen?" asks Mrs. Patel.

"It's nothing bad." It's the opposite of bad.

Jana's eyes grow wide. "You—"

"Shh," I say. "Later."

Mrs. Patel switches to an all-news station, and Jana shrugs like *why not now?* since the news is on. But I shake my head again. There's no way I'm going to talk about my crush in front of Jana's mom. She's so proper, it'd freak her out. She's the kind of person who vacuums her car each week so it keeps that new smell. Plus, if I say I have a crush, she might tell my parents. For all I know, Mrs. Patel knows Jacob's parents. She's the administrator at the local hospital and knows everyone.

We're passing by the shopping center. An SUV full of some girls that Katie knows from ballet waves at our van. But we only half-heartedly wave back. That's because the girl in the front seat is Fiona Callum. She used to be one of Jana's BFFs and sat with us at lunch—until she betrayed Jana. Now we all pretty much can't stand her. After what she did, she deserves it.

A few more turns and we'll be at school and then it'll be safe to talk.

"Girls, bad news," Mrs. Patel says. "There's construction up ahead on Church Street."

"You could turn around. I know an alternative route," says Katie, the human map.

"Can't turn around," says Mrs. Patel. "It's just one lane."

"Are we going to be late?" asks Torielle. In addition to her beautiful singing voice and love of movies, she's famous for her perfect attendance record.

"I think we'll make it, but just barely." Mrs. Patel shakes her head. "Really, today? They have to start construction on the first day of school?"

Finally, after being stopped for what feels like forever, we get through the one-lane traffic as Mrs. Patel continues a running monologue about the town's lack of common sense. A bunch of boys on bikes whiz past the minivan; unfortunately, none of them are Jacob. Finally, we enter the twenty-five-mile-an-hour school zone.

"Good news, girls," says Mrs. Patel. "We're going to make it just on time!"

The school looms at the end of the block. A sign outside with those moveable letters says WELCOME BACK TO SCHOOL! A line of cars wait to turn into the circular drive in front of the school while other cars park a couple of blocks away.

We pull up to the drop-off circle.

"Doesn't school look smaller than it did last year?" I say. "Like it shrank in the heat of the summer?"

"Spoken just like an artist," says Katie in a flat voice. I can't tell if it's a compliment or an insult. Sometimes being the quieter one in a group of stars, I worry I don't belong.

"I think Maddie's right," says Jana, and it feels like she's jumping to my defense. I instantly love her even more. "The school does look weenie."

"I think it's because we're just older and more mature," says Torielle in a fake sophisticated voice.

"Yes, we're very ooh-la-la," says Katie.

Snorting with laughter, we hop out of the van and shuffle onto the sidewalk as Mrs. Patel wishes us a great first day of school. Clumps of seventh and eighth graders stand in front of the school, laughing and talking to each other. Some people are comparing schedules, which we got in the mail last week. You can spot the sixth graders because they look a little lost or they're walking in with their parents. There's a sign-up table for parents to join the PTA, and they're giving out donuts to the ones who sign up. The air smells sweet and powdery, and suddenly I'm feeling hungry—I barely ate any breakfast. I always get nervous the first day of school. Sort of the same feeling I get in airports before I'm about to go someplace. Queasy, but a good kind of queasy.

There's lot of hugging from the girls, and the boys are all glancing around and elbowing each other. Some of the boys kick hacky sacks back and forth, while others lean against the cinderblock wall that's covered in a mural about recycling, staring at their phones.

As soon as Mrs. Patel pulls away, Jana pokes me on my shoulder, "So tell us what happened, Maddie."

"Yeah," says Katie as we wander toward the covered picnic table area, where groups of mostly seventh graders are hanging out.

"What is it?" asks Torielle.

Picturing Jacob, I feel the smile stretch across my face, and say, "Well . . ." when the bell rings.

"Tell us later," says Torielle. "Don't want to be late."

"Definitely not," says Katie, smoothing down her already neat bangs. "It's the first day."

We say goodbye and turn down different hallways because, unfortunately, we all have different advisories. Which is so unfair! It's like the administration is out to make us miss each other!

Then, out of the corner of my eye, I see Jacob walking in another direction. His hair falls perfectly across his forehead. Pivoting, he waves at me before he turns around the corner.

I sigh deeply as I pass by a bulletin board advertising the club sign-ups. Yes, I might be sighing all the way through advisory and straight into lunch.

Chapter Five:
TWINS

"Sorry you were stuck at home all Labor Day weekend," says Jana, coming out of the stall. We're in the bathroom with Katie, getting ready to head into the cafeteria.

"It wasn't that bad," I admit, washing my hands. In a minute or two I'm going to tell my friends why.

One word: Jacob.

"The cabin was fun," says Jana, "but even nature can get a little boring."

"My weekend was definitely un-boring." I'm feeling as light and frothy as whipped cream right now, like the world is as sweet as a sip of pumpkin spice frappé at the Friendly Bean. I can feel the full effect of my crush buzzing through me. Just seeing Jacob for a microsecond before advisory did the trick.

Katie's shoes click on the tiles. She stands next to me in front of the mirror. "My hair's crazy today," she complains.

Actually, her hair looks exactly the same as usual. It's shoulder-length, blond, and straight. I would love to have hair that always looks the same. But it doesn't—every day, it fluffs in a different direction. I take a look at my face in the mirror. Almond-shaped hazel eyes. A few freckles on my nose, and dark brown hair. My mom's family is Cuban, and I actually get the freckles from both her side and my dad's. She grew up in Miami after her parents moved from Cuba. Then she went to college up in New England, which is where she met my dad, whose family has lived in Massachusetts for a while. They're Scottish and Irish, but way back from a long time ago. My dad has a whole collection of silly shirts that say *Got Kilt?* and stuff like that. I get my height from him—he's six foot three. I'm tall for a seventh grader, though Mom swears everyone will catch up soon.

Jana, Katie, and I zip out into the hall together. I

fling my arms around their shoulders, which is something Jana would usually do. But I'm feeling peppy right now. It's perfect timing for a drumroll moment. I open my mouth to say, "Guess what?"

But just then, Jana squeals and turns around. "Okay, I have news. Big news."

"What?" asks Katie.

Torielle bounds up to our group. "You better spill," she says, grinning. I notice she's got aqua blue braces on today. I hadn't noticed in the car. Torielle can make anything look good.

"We're waiting," says Torielle.

"Okay," gushes Jana. "For math, I have Mrs. Keener, who is soooo hard."

"That's news?" Torielle shakes her head. "Everyone knows that. But she's really good. And will prepare you for algebra next year." Torielle would know. She's skipped ahead in math.

"It's not the teacher part," says Jana as we walk up the cafeteria double doors. "It's who's *in* Mrs. Keener's class." She pauses dramatically and lowers her voice. "My new crush." We pause in front of the caf entrance because there's a mob of kids in front of us.

"Really?" I say eagerly. I can't believe Jana and I

have crushes at the same time. But of course, we do. We're BFFs.

Katie laughs. "Well, it's about time for you to have a new crush, Jana. It's about two weeks since you were going on and on about Alfred, that basketball player."

"Arnie," corrects Jana, pushing through the double doors. We follow her in.

"So, who is it?" I ask.

We stroll into the cafeteria, looking around for an empty table. We like the round ones, because they're smaller and you can't be surprised by unwelcome or annoying visitors. "Okay," says Jana. "Turn your eyes over to the Quik Cart." That's a cart where you can buy healthy food like bananas and yogurt.

We all pause, scanning for the Quik Cart. A cafeteria worker walks past carrying a fresh tray of sliced carrots for the salad bar. "See that guy who just sat down?" says Jana.

"Um, there's probably like a hundred boys who just sat down," says Torielle.

"But not over here," says Jana. "Oh, let's grab this table—hurry up!"

She plops down at a round table to our left before a boy with a SpongeBob t-shirt can nab it.

"Describe," I say, sitting down in a chair next to Jana. Torielle sits on the other side of her, and Katie takes the seat next to Torielle. I place my lunch bag onto the table and pull out a thermos of soup. "In more detail." I unscrew the lid, and steam from chicken rice soup puffs into my face. It smells delicious. Mom made it in honor of the first day of school. "We want to know more!" I take a spoonful.

"The ridiculously cute one," gushes Jana. She pulls her sandwich out of her lunch sack. "With amazing blue eyes and curly brownish-reddish hair." I whirl around, scanning the tables for someone who meets that description. "His name's Jacob," she adds. "And he's new."

I blink and feel lightheaded, but not in a good way. In an I'm-going-to-faint way. I drop my spoon with a clatter onto the table, but nobody notices. They are too busy staring at an extremely cute boy.

An extremely cute and very familiar boy.

"See!" says Jana, like she's cheering on our team at a soccer game. "He's wearing a blue shirt." She might be saying something else but I'm not hearing.

He isn't just any Jacob.

He's *my* Jacob.

"He's cute, right?" asks Jana.

"Uh kind of," I squeak. If she likes Jacob, he'll be sure to like her back. Boys always do. She's so much fun and athletic and outgoing. And good at flirting. She's the center of the orbit—honestly, the rest of us circulate around her. He probably will too.

"Kind of?" says Torielle. She waves a hand in front of my face. "Are you blinded by the fluorescent lights or something?"

A group of band kids tromps past me, swinging their instruments, and a clarinet almost smacks into my side.

"He's really nice too," gushes Jana. "And funny."

Yeah, I know that. I blink, staring at the taco bar, specifically the shredded lettuce bin. Because I can't look at Jacob, not now that he's *Jana's* Jacob.

It's so unfair.

A few girls squeeze past our table carrying their lunch trays loaded up with slices of pizza. The smell of the cheese makes my stomach twist. Jana is talking on and on about Jacob like she's some Jacob expert. Like she's got a PhD in all things Jacob.

"And he plays goalie for a platinum traveling team, the Rattlers," she's saying.

I didn't know that part. How does she already know

more? I push away my thermos of soup. There's just no way I can eat it now.

"He's pretty perfect for you if he's good at soccer," says Katie enthusiastically. She bites into her salad. And I'm feeling like Katie is low-key sucking up to Jana.

On our soccer team, I'm a defender, but I'm just okay. Jana, on the other hand, is the star midfielder. She scores, she defends. She does it all. I mainly warm the bench. I'm really good at that.

"I know," Jana is saying in her loud voice over the babble of the cafeteria. "He's tall. I'm short. We both have names that start with J. And the soccer thing—I can practice shooting on him. It's sooo perfect."

Torielle puts an arm around Jana. "Okay, girls, this means that by the BFF Code, Jacob is now officially off limits."

Katie pokes Jana in the shoulder. "Luckily, Jacob's a troll, so you can have him. Ha, ha."

"In the name of the BFF Code of Honor," Jana jokes back, "I thank you for letting me have my troll all to myself."

I want a hole to open up in the caf floor and just swallow me. Take me to some world where Jana does not know Jacob. Where they're not perfect for each other.

Where Jana is allergic to soccer balls and bright blue eyes.

Where the star midfielder can't practice shooting on the star goalie.

Sick. I'm really going to be sick.

Jana snaps her fingers in front of my eyes. I don't even blink. I'm not sure I'm exactly breathing. I'm sure I look paler than the cottage cheese at the salad bar.

"Hello, Maddie, are you there?" Now it's Torielle snapping her fingers in my face.

"Uh, yes. I was thinking about . . . all the homework I have already."

"Really?" Jana laughs. "Since when do you think about homework?" It's true. I'm not exactly like Elvie. Even the rest of my friends are more into school than me.

Katie leans in. "Maddie, you had something to tell us too. Remember?"

I freeze. Can I tell them?

"You promised," says Torielle, wiping her hand on a napkin.

My lips feel dry. My throat feels like I've swallowed the entire plum in my lunch sack.

If Jana likes a boy, he always likes her back. My crush is now pointless. And completely against the BFF Code of Honor. But I could at least tell Jana that I saw him first and thought he was crush-worthy.

"There's something else," I say. "It's about Jacob."

But then at the table kitty-corner from us, I spot Fiona Callum. With her pale, white-blond hair and her oval-shaped face and oval-shaped glasses. She sits with her new friends, who apparently don't mind sitting with someone who can't keep secrets. Someone who blabs.

Fiona the Betrayer. That's what we all call her.

Jana's ex–best friend. Last year, she told everyone that Jana lied about her bra size and was using padding. It was just so mean.

And a week later, Jana had cut herself shaving her underarm and she was really embarrassed about it. So she had put a Band-Aid on it and said that she was cut while rock climbing with her family. But Fiona posted a photo of Jana shaving her underarm, and wrote the real reason that Jana was wearing a Band-Aid. Again, so evil.

Out of loyalty, none of us will talk to Fiona.

I can't become that girl. I can't become a Betrayer and an ex–best friend. A lump grows in my throat. If I don't say anything at all about Jacob, I prevent the possibility of being a traitor. I know what happens when you go against Jana. Like Fiona, I'd get totally cut off.

Anyway, there's no way I could hurt Jana. She is my *very* best friend. She'd seriously do anything for me. She never leaves me out, and she always sticks up for me. Even when I just get my seven minutes of playing time on the soccer field, she's the one cheering me on the loudest.

Anyway, she's Jana. She'll grow out of her crush. She always does. Like Katie says, just give her a week.

"What about Jacob?" asks Jana, her forehead furrows in worry. She balls up her napkin.

"It's just . . . that . . . with his curly hair and tallness and bright eyes, it'd be really fun to draw a picture of him for you," I say in what I hope is an enthusiastic voice.

"Awesome," says Jana.

"Yes, awesome," I say, swallowing the lump in my throat that just grew a whole lot bigger.

Chapter Six:
Keep Calm

I'm still feeling queasy after lunch as Jana and I stroll into Social Studies. It's one of the few classes we have together. History posters, timelines, and banners plaster the walls. They say things like:

DEBATE: TWO SIDES TO EVERY STORY
KEEP CALM AND DEBATE ON
SOCIAL STUDIES ROCKS!
CHANGE THE WORLD. LEARN HISTORY.

"I can't believe how many posters Ms. Yoon has," I murmur to Jana over the chatter in the room.

"It's seriously like an art gallery," she agrees.

Some kids stand around chatting while others sit down at desks. Ms. Yoon is tall and has long dark hair with one pinkish streak.

"Hi, Jana!" calls out Fiona from across the room.

"Hey, Fiona," Jana says in a flat voice. She waves, but under her breath she says in an irritated voice, "Great. *She's* in this class."

Fiona wears jeans and a hoodie, even though it's not cold. She dresses in a casual sporty way, sort of like how Jana used to dress before she got a little more fashionable under Torielle's influence.

Fiona smiles at Jana as if they are long-lost family, which I guess they kind of are. Fiona completely confuses me. How could she be so callous to Jana one year and then feel like she can say hello to her as if nothing happened? Actually, I feel embarrassed for Fiona. She's trying so hard. Can't she tell that there's no way that Jana is ever going to forgive her? I've heard both Torielle and Katie talk about it. Once Jana's your friend, she'd give away her last dollar to you. But if you cross her, watch out!

Two boys strut into the room, and Jana's eyes grow big. One of them is Landon Linklater, and the other is Jacob. Jacob waves and sits with Landon in the back row. I feel my face getting warm.

Jana lowers her voice. "Jacob's such a wall when it comes to goalie. Last year, in one game, he made thirty-three saves."

"Oh," I say. "You already know so much about him." I feel a flicker of irritation. Even if he's now officially her crush, I met him first.

"I mostly have just heard a lot about him," Jana says.

"Really? From who?" I ask.

"Fiona."

"Does she like him too?"

Jana shakes her head. "Eww, no—she's his cousin."

"Oh, right. I think I heard that." I have not actually heard that.

"I'm Ms. Yoon," says our teacher, who has just finished writing on the whiteboard. "We'll start in a few minutes." Ms. Yoon looks super young, like maybe she recently graduated from college. She wears jeans and a really pretty red cable-knit sweater. Her hair shines in the lights as if she's a model in a shampoo ad.

A lot of kids are already seated, and a couple of latecomers stream in carrying their backpacks.

Something smells chocolaty but I can't tell where it's coming from. As the classroom fills up, I get a stomach-jumpy feeling. It's because Jacob is so close.

Out of the corner of my eye, so that I'm not obvious, I sneak a glance at him. He's opening his binder. And that's when I know I have to stop liking him. At least for now. Until Jana stops liking him.

Ms. Yoon strolls around the classroom and nods as the bell rings.

"Looks like it's time to start class. I'm so ridiculously excited to start our year!" Ms. Yoon pulls a screen down over the whiteboard and grabs a remote. "Could someone turn off the lights?"

"I will!" yells Bryce Pisani from across the room. He practically jumps over a desk to turn off the lights.

Ms. Yoon clicks on a photo of the Romans clad in armor. "How many people think history is boring?"

A few kids raise their hands.

"Don't be shy," she says. "You can admit it."

More kids raise their hands. Next she explains that not only are we going to study the past, but we are going to debate it. That we will look at primary and secondary resources.

"It doesn't matter if you don't know what I mean yet—soon you will. While there will be some individual work, this year is going to be mostly project-based learning, or PBL," she explains. "That means that for much of the time we're going to work in groups. One of the main ways we'll look at history is to debate various topics, everything from 'Why did Rome Fall?' to 'The Effectiveness of the Justinian Code."

"What's that?" asks a girl in the back.

"You'll find out soon enough." Ms. Yoon flashes a slide of a statue. "This is Julius Caesar, a ruler of Ancient Rome. In this class, you're not just going to read about him. Later on this semester, you're going to *be* him."

"Is this an acting class, or Social Studies?" I whisper, shaking my head.

Jana shrugs, but I can tell she's thinking it sounds neat. Jana doesn't have a shy bone in her body.

Ms. Yoon projects a photo of a student wearing a toga and a wreath. Everyone laughs. "Don't laugh, because that's going to be you," she says. "Well, only if you pick Julius Caesar as your Roman historical figure. There will be many to choose from." She clicks through to another slide, and it all it says is "Debate is fun!"

A few people shake their heads, including me.

"It's okay for you to be dubious," says Ms. Yoon. "Most of you haven't tried it. The first thing we're going to do is learn how to debate. And in order to do that I'm going to assign you debate groups."

My hand shoots up, and Ms. Yoon nods at me. "Does everyone in the group have to debate, or could we just do the research?"

"Everyone has to debate," she says, scanning the classroom. "Each and every one of you. No exceptions."

I hold in a groan, and Jana gives me a sympathetic smile. Still, I know she's not worried. That's why she's captain of our soccer team. My shoulders tense just thinking about speaking in front of everyone.

"You're going to learn basic debating techniques," says Ms. Yoon, "such as the presentation of your main argument and how to create a rebuttal. And when it comes to the actual debate, you won't be memorizing speeches or reading aloud already-written scripts—just glancing at your notes."

We can't read anything? I'm starting to feel not so great. If I have to speak in front of people without even writing it out beforehand, there's no way I can get a good grade in this class. Everyone is going to see me crash and burn.

But Ms. Yoon looks super excited. She's speaking in an enthusiastic voice about how we'll use our knowledge in the moment while we're debating. She makes wide gestures with her arms. "It's going to be all about teamwork, research, and fun! And did I mention fun? On our special debate days, we'll bring in snacks like popcorn and cookies. It'll be a party!"

A bunch of girls clap and even stomp their feet. Really? They actually think that would be fun?

"In this class, we even have some members of the debate team, such as Fiona Callum." Fiona gives a little fist pump into the air. "And Keisha Tinsley." Keisha waves. "I'm hoping that you will all love debate so much you will join the team too," says Ms. Yoon.

Not likely. As in, *never*! That's the very last thing I would ever do.

Ms. Yoon puts her hand to her forehead as if she's a sailor gazing at the sea. "Maybe a few of you debaters, those of you who have participated on the debate team, could stand up and say a little about it."

The first person to stand up is Fiona. Her hoodie has a picture of a clarinet on it. Underneath it says *I play well*—which seems so conceited to me! "Even if you think you can't debate, you can," she says smugly.

"You might have to work for it, but debating can give you superpowers." She smiles widely so you can see her full set of braces. What a show-off.

Then Ms. Yoon calls on Jacob, and my heart hiccups, even though my mind says I don't care about him.

He moves forward from the back of the classroom. It's crazy, but I can feel his nearness, even though I don't turn my head to look at him when he brushes past. He starts to talk, shaking his mop of gorgeous hair out of his eyes as he speaks.

Jana is staring straight at him.

I'm trying to be more subtle and sneak glances. Jacob puts his hands in his pockets and rises on the balls of his feet. "I'm Jacob. I'm new. But I already know a lot of people here. And in case you didn't know, Fiona is my cousin, so debate runs in the genes." He looks at her and grins, and she gives him a big thumbs-up. "At my old school I debated. It was fun. You get to bang on the desks and stuff." Jacob makes it sound better than Fiona does. Maybe because he makes it more of a joke. Fiona isn't exactly known for her sense of humor.

Jana arches her eyebrows significantly and cups her hand to whisper to me, "He's smart too."

My stomach lurches. I don't like him being even more perfect.

Then another girl, Risa Cappeto, raises her hand and comes to the front of the class. She has short black hair and really fun-looking purple glasses. "Last year I was afraid to debate and do public speaking. I thought maybe I wasn't good enough. But I am good enough. Now I want to be a lawyer when I grow up. So if any of you are afraid, that's normal."

Being afraid is definitely normal for me. What are all the things I would do if I wasn't afraid? I don't really like to think about it. Maybe quit soccer.

Ms. Yoon says the first thing we will do is form teams of four, and then break into partners. Each partner group will work together to research and prepare for our first debate. She explains how important it will be for everyone to contribute and work cooperatively. To get used to debating, she will give us current event topics for the first debate. But in the future, we will be debating historical stuff like the fall of Rome.

I glance at Jana, who looks back and says under her breath, "I hope we get to work together."

"Me too," I say, crossing my fingers.

"Or I get to work with Jacob." Jana winks and nudges her chin toward the back of the classroom, where Jacob is sitting.

As if she can read our minds, Maya Kusuma raises her hand. "Can we pick who we work with?" she asks, and glances knowingly at Keisha, who already looks like she is a lawyer ready to speak in front of a judge. "I really want to work with someone I know."

Ms. Yoon says, "If there's someone you'd really like to work with, please write it down and I'll take it into consideration. It doesn't guarantee you'll work together, though."

I write down my name and then Jana. Ms. Yoon comes around and collects our preferences.

"Okay, moving on to creating our classroom contract," says Ms. Yoon enthusiastically, and we dive into that. We agree that it's okay to make mistakes because that is how you figure stuff out. We also pledge to work together and respect one another. Then Ms. Yoon has all of the class members sign the contract.

"Sure, it's a little cheesy," says Ms. Yoon. Some kids laugh. "But it's useful. Sometimes getting things in writing helps."

I feel a small pang. If only this class were just writing, I'd be okay with that. But I have a feeling I'm about to make a big fool out of myself in Social Studies this year.

The bell rings and I overhear Fiona say in an obnoxiously loud voice, "This class is going to be so much fun!"

"Really?" I say under my breath to Jana. "Getting your braces tightened would be fun compared to being forced to do a debate."

As we're leaving, Jacob walks by and says hi. After he's a safe distance away, Jana puts her hand over her heart. "My heart is racing. He's a public health risk."

He sure is, I think. It's going to be hard not liking him.

Somehow, throughout the rest of the day, I'm able to push away any Jacob thoughts. In my other classes, I focus on taking very neat notes and creating elaborate doodles of my classmates. I notice all kinds of things, like how the linoleum floor has yellow and gray flecks in it—which are not our school colors, but our rival middle school's colors. And how nobody stuffs their oversized backpacks in the metal baskets under the desks because they're too small, and thus pointless. My plan seems to be working. I'm very busy noticing my Jacob-free surroundings.

When school ends, Jana and I make our way to the bus pick-up area. Kids crowd the hallway, especially the sixth graders, who bunch together in groups and jostle us. Still, I'm feeling calm and happy to be with my best friend now that classes are over. We're not walking, exactly, but doing this bump-skip thing. And giggling. It's more fun to be with Jana than anyone I know.

She slows down in front of the birthday bulletin board by the office. "I want to see my name."

"And you should," I point out. The birthday bulletin board is a giant board that lists the names of students who have a birthday each month, and the date of their birthday. Every month there are at least fifty names.

We both scan the board. "There you are," I say. "See. Jana Patel, September sixteenth."

Jana claps her hands over her mouth. "Oh. My. Gosh."

"What?" I ask, alarmed. A bunch of sixth graders streak past us, yelling.

Jana shakes her head.

"Seriously, Jana. Tell me."

"Look who's almost right next to me," she says.

My eyes scan and stop on a familiar name. Jacob Matthews. My heart starts pattering. Shoot! I thought I had purged myself of any Jacob feelings. Ha, ha.

"Jacob and I are September birthday buddies!" she shrieks. "Look, his is on September tenth!"

"Wow," I say, trying to sound excited for her.

She jumps up and down, hanging onto my sleeve. "Can you believe it?"

No. Just another thing that unites them. "That's awesome," I say, with a sinking feeling. We make our way outside to the drive-in circle where the buses wait. There are mobs of kids looking for buses or waving at parents. I feel like the world is conspiring to bring my crush and my best friend together. And for me to keep on thinking about it.

"Maybe Jacob and I could have double parties," says Jana, grinning.

"Ha, ha."

"I know. It's not like we've spoken *that* much yet. Speaking of parties, did I tell you that my mom said we can rent a karaoke machine for my sleepover? And do the nail salon in the family room, as long as I put a cloth down first over the carpet? Mom's worried I'm going to drip polish over her new Berber rug. She said she'd give me money to go to the store to pick out colors."

"Wow. And the karaoke machine!" That's going to be cool. I'm back to being excited. First of all, Jana loves to sing duets with me, even though she's usually out of key. I can't sing either, except in the shower. My voice is kind of warbly. So together, we're so bad it's awesome.

"Plus, my dad will make homemade pizzas in our brick oven. And we can all choose our toppings."

"That sounds like so much fun!"

"I know. My mom even said that since I'm turning thirteen, she'll let us stay up past midnight." That was a big deal for Mrs. Patel. She's a sleep fanatic. Everyone has sleep shades, and she doesn't let Jana get exposed to any blue light from her computer or phone after eight o'clock. Like I said, strict.

"I can't wait!" I say.

Jana grins as we part ways. "See you at practice!"

"Yes," I said. "See you."

Somehow Jana had actually convinced me to join the soccer team last year. Even though I don't really like how you have to scream on the field sometimes, and how when you're a defender you basically have to use your body as a human shield. At least being a defender is better than being a midfielder, like Jana. She loves it, but they have to run around. A lot. As a defender, I do have to run and even steal the ball, but not as much as a midfielder.

Anyway, I had done youth soccer when I was little. But I just wasn't one of those soccer girls, so I had quit. But then Jana said it was so much fun doing traveling soccer—you got to go to tournaments like the Boo Fest and wear Halloween costumes.

I remember exactly when I gave in last spring. As we had hurried down the hallway before first period that day, she had begged, "C'mon, Maddie. Please. Just do it. At least try out. It'll be fun."

"I won't know anyone," I had insisted.

"You know me. Isn't that enough?" She smiled.

"I'll think about it," I said. Which was a mistake, because it gave her a wide opening.

She kept up her pestering all day, and, finally, I just gave up resisting. Plus, if I'm being honest, I'll admit that I wanted something more to do after school, since my ceramics class was only once a week.

My best friend could convince anyone of anything. She had once pleaded with our math teacher, Mrs. Pearson, not to give her a zero for missing homework. Jana told her that red sauce had splattered on her homework and that her poodle, Gus, had eaten the assignment. Mrs. Pearson smiled at her and said not to worry. If I had told that story, Mrs. Pearson would have definitely marked down a zero. But instead, Mrs. Pearson actually put down a check plus in her online grade book for Jana, and asked if she did any dog sitting. It was unbelievable.

Sometimes I wish I could talk like Jana—to say whatever I wanted, and have everyone listen.

Once I get back home, I think about how today was a very surprising first day of school. But even with everything that happened, I'm still really looking forward to Jana's birthday.

While Morty jumps up and licks me, my mom peppers me with a thousand questions about how the day went. She's never satisfied with "fine." She wants details.

Elvie always gives her details, so I try. I tell her a little bit about my Science teacher, Mr. Gibson, who was wearing purple socks and has red frizzy hair and a big bushy beard. I tell her how this year I didn't forget my locker combination and knew exactly where to go. I tell her that Social Studies will be very interesting, but I don't tell her about Jana's crush. And I don't tell her about mine. I mean, my not-crush.

I'm feeling pretty confused about the crush problem. I even flip through a few of Mom's self-help books, but I can't say that they have answers. One of them says "Be your own best friend." I'm not really sure how that would help. Because if I were being my own best friend, I'd tell myself all about Jacob.

Later, when Elvie gets home from high school, she excitedly shows me a list of books she's going to be reading in AP Literature. We're upstairs in the atrium office and we're both about to start our schoolwork. "The teacher is incredible," she says. "We're going to be doing in-class timed writing prompts all year."

"Really? That doesn't sound like fun."

Elvie plops down on a chair in front of her computer. "Mrs. King is going to show us all of these techniques. Apparently, almost everyone who takes her class gets fours and fives on the AP exam. She's really hard, but it's going to be worth it."

She immediately goes to YouTube and brings up a video showing a lesson on how to play the electric bass. Confused, I stare at the video. "But you don't even have an electric bass." Elvie's upright bass sits downstairs in the living room, in the corner behind the piano. She usually practices it after dinner or sometimes even before school.

"I'm going to get an electric bass," she declares, moving her fingers like she's playing air guitar. I mean, air bass. "And start my own band."

"How are you going to have time for that and playing upright bass, with all your clubs and AP classes?"

"You sound just like Mom and Dad," says Elvie, sighing.

I pop my hand over my mouth. "I do. Wow. I did not mean that."

"It's okay," she says, looking at me proudly. "You're growing up."

Chapter Seven:
The Reminder

The next day I tuck my phone into my pocket and enter through the double doors into the cafeteria. It's already jam-packed, and the hot lunch line is practically all the way to the taco bar. Jana and Torielle find me, and we make our way to the middle of the cafeteria, where Katie is at a table by the Fixings Bar. (That's the place where you can get packets of ketchup, mustard, salt, pepper, and extra napkins.)

I turn my head and catch Jacob's eye. He's sitting with a couple of soccer boys in the back of the cafeteria next to the Quik Cart. He waves over at us. I nod and smile. Torielle taps Jana on the shoulder.

"Jacob's saying something to you," says Torielle

to Jana. Actually, I think he was waving at me, but I don't say anything.

"Oh, hey," mouths Jana breezily as she turns to wave enthusiastically. I wave, too, since I don't want to be rude.

"It's a good sign, right?" Jana asks.

"Very," I say, and stop waving.

"Maddie, I didn't know you knew him," Jana says.

"Um, he's in Social Studies with us," I point out.

"Right." Jana takes a bite out of her turkey sandwich. "I guess he's just friendly."

"Exactly."

"Don't you think he waved longer than necessary at me?" she asks.

"I guess so."

Katie opens her lime-green lunch bag and pulls out a matching lime-green napkin, which she lays out on the table after blowing all the crumbs away. "FYI. Whether you guys like it or not, I've signed you up to work at the Halloween Haunted House fundraiser that the PTA is sponsoring in October."

"Yes please," says Torielle. "That was so fun last year."

"Agreed," I say.

"There's nothing like scaring people." Jana curls her hands like claws and bares her teeth, making a crazy face. We all giggle.

"Just give me some ideas for the back-to-school faculty luncheon," says Katie. "My mom, Miss PTA president, has been bugging me about what the teachers will like."

"Pizza?" suggests Torielle.

"No." Katie shakes her head. "That's a kid thing."

"Then lasagna," says Jana.

"Okay, that could work." Katie places some sushi rolls, pumpkin seeds, and a pear onto her cloth napkin. "Or maybe not. What if we did something unexpected? Like maybe pizza rolls, but gourmet. With wedges of fresh mozzarella?"

I set down my thermos of soup and fold my arms. "Why unexpected?"

"Because it's a fun surprise," says Jana. "Every-one loves surprises."

Really? Personally, I'm tired of surprises. This week has been too unexpected already.

Then something funny happens to Katie's eyes; they grow strangely big. "Yes, pizza rolls," she says, slowing down her speech. "They. Are. Very. Delicious."

"I agree," says Torielle, in an equally strained and slow voice. "And *very* cute." She's acting oddly, leaning back in her chair and sort of nodding backwards. "And nearby."

"What's up with you guys?" says Jana.

"I know," I say with a laugh. "You two are acting so weird."

"Behind you and approaching," hisses Torielle, "At six o'clock." She's into detective movies and loves to sound like one sometimes.

"*Jacob*," Katie breathes. "He's walking over here with Lukas Wu."

Jana's mouth drops open.

My mouth drops open.

We turn around, and the boys are right there.

"Oh, hi again!" I say a little too loudly, and Jana does the same.

"How's it going over here?" asks Jacob.

"Great!" says Jana.

"Awesome," says Jacob.

Am I crazy, or do his eyes linger on mine? He gives his signature Jacob lopsided grin. But I decide to be immune to it.

Jana introduces him to Torielle and Katie. We

already know Lukas, but it feels like we're meeting him for the first time. He's popular with the boys but somewhat quiet around girls.

Jacob eyes the two empty seats at our table. He's wearing a bright blue shirt, the same color as his eyes. "Are these seats taken?" he asks, all casual.

"No!" says Jana, probably too enthusiastically.

Lukas sits down in the empty chair next to me. Jacob sits down right next to Jana. Lukas is nice—a little short, but cute, and he has spiky, short dark brown hair. He always wears these FC Barcelona t-shirts and he's famous for his ability to juggle. I mean in soccer, where you bounce the ball from knee to knee, or to your head—or to anywhere but your hands. He's as good as Jana.

"I love creamy spinach," says Lukas. He points to a pool of something green in his tray.

"Seriously?" I'm not sure what to say to that. This is the first time—*ever*—that boys have eaten with us. This makes us the first table to officially eat with boys. Last year, some guys would stop by our table. Okay, more like throw napkins at the back of our heads or jog past and swipe cookies. But this feels different because they're not here to prank us. I feel like the eyes of the entire seventh grade are on us right now, especially Fiona's. She can't like Jacob because, eww, he's her cousin, so I think she's staring at Lukas. And because he's next to me, she's staring at me so hard, I feel like she's going to burn a hole into my forehead.

"So . . ." Jacob raises his eyebrows and looks at me innocently. "Do they have any coffee machines in the caf?"

"No," I blurt. "Only in the teacher's lounge." I try to think of something to redirect the conversation. I haven't told Jana about our Friendly Bean encounter, and it would be so awkward for it to come up now! In desperation, I reach for a spork behind me at the Fixings Bar.

"Too bad," says Jacob. "Because I—"

"Can you believe someone thought this was a good idea?" I say, holding up the spork.

"No," says Lukas, rolling his eyes. "That'd never work for creamy spinach!"

"Neither fork nor spoon," says Katie.

"I forgot about their existence." Jacob pulls a mini Snickers bar out of his lunch bag. Apparently, he eats dessert first. "We didn't have sporks in my old school." And suddenly I'm smiling because Jacob is talking about sporks and not coffee. He's nowhere near talking about pumpkin spice frappé. Phew!

Katie takes a bite of her pear. "Don't you think one day they could purchase an actual utensil? I might ask the PTA about that."

"What, like a fork?" says Torielle. Soon the awkwardness evaporates when we start arguing about other sorts of utensils we could invent. "Cupknife" was axed, as was the "spray," a giant spoon that's also a tray.

"Lunch got better with Jacob and Lukas there," says Katie, which surprises me, since I thought she would mind having boys at our table. We're heading down the hall to our fifth-period class.

"Seriously better," adds Torielle, as we brush past a knot of sixth graders who are still looking a bit lost, even though it's no longer the first day.

"Yes!" Jana and I say at the same time. "Jinx!" we both cry out. "You can't speak until someone says your name!" And we both laugh but then close our mouths and make hand signals instead of talking the rest of the way down the hall.

After we say goodbye to Torielle and Katie, who both have Language Arts together, Jana and I go to Social Studies.

"What's so funny?" asks Fiona as we walk into class. "Tell me, you guys," she begs.

I can't believe she's still trying to interact with Jana.

But we both tap our chests. We are so desperate to talk that both of us want Fiona to say our names.

"You're crazy," says Fiona. In that moment, I'm not a very nice person—I really would like to slap Fiona. We're not crazy. We're just two best friends having fun. Fiona is the crazy one. She embarrassed Jana just to try to score some points on social media.

Still, we both nod and continue to tap our chests.

"I don't understand you, Maddie and Jana!" Fiona says.

"Thank you," bursts out Jana, hugging Fiona. Wow. That was strange. She really did that? Hugged the Betrayer? Did I hallucinate? And then it hits me—Fiona is Jacob's cousin. Maybe Jana wants to get close to Fiona again to get close to Jacob.

"Thank you," I say, still irritated that Jana was so quick to hug Fiona. "Not being able to talk in Social Studies would have been a real problem."

Chapter Eight:
The Debate

Today, we're getting our debate topics in Social Studies.

I know because Ms. Yoon has just written on the whiteboard in giant orange letters:

Today: Debate Topics!!!

I shrug off my backpack and sit down. I'm not exactly happy about this.

The bell hasn't rung yet, but it's about to any second. Chatter fills the room as kids make their way inside. All around me, students unzip their backpacks and slap their binders onto their desks, reminding me that I'm going to have to debate in front of all of them. Ugh! Public speaking is my worst nightmare. I know I'll be cringe-y bad. When I get nervous I start to talk really fast. I sweat and my voice gets shaky.

I race up to Ms. Yoon. "Would it be possible to do an independent study?" I ask. Actually, I'm more like begging.

"There are always all kinds of possibilities," she says, putting away her dry-erase marker on the ledge. "What interests you?"

"I'm not sure. I want to do something to replace the debate."

"I'm sorry, Maddie, but everyone has to debate. That's not something you can get out of."

"All right," I say, trying to look more cheerful than I feel. More kids flow into the room, and the bell is about to ring. I sit back down.

"What were you talking to Ms. Yoon about?" Jana asks, turning around in the desk in front of mine. I explain, and she gives me a sympathetic look.

"It's so hot in here." She fans her face. Her cheeks are apple red.

"I know. It's like a sauna." I might not be happy about having to do public speaking, but at least my best friend sits nearby. I really hate the fact that we don't have any morning classes together. It's so unfair. At least Ms. Yoon is one of those cool teachers who lets students sit where they want. Not-so-nice teachers use alphabetical order. My last name is Campbell, which means I always have to sit next to Fiona Callum in my other classes. She talks endlessly about how she and Jana did this or that when they used to be best friends. It's super annoying.

Jana sneaks a glance behind us, where Jacob sits in the last row with Lukas.

"Jacob's soooo cute," she whispers. It's true. Even if I'm not supposed to notice it. He and Lukas are batting a hacky sack back and forth, and somehow Ms. Yoon isn't noticing.

I school my features. "I'm going to have splash some cold water on your face," I joke, "to cool you down."

"As long as it's not the nasty warm water from the fountain," says Jana with a groan.

"Don't worry. The water fountains are always blocked up from all the spit wads and gum. So it will have both gum and spit in it."

"Eww." Jana makes one of her silly faces. She goes cross-eyed and puckers her lips.

I giggle. She really knows how to make the best faces. It's one of the many reasons why I love her. I feel proud of myself for holding up my end of the BFF Code and staying neutral when it comes to Jacob. But how much longer can I keep this up? Hopefully, I won't have to for much longer. I'm sure Jana will flip flop to a new crush like she always does.

At the front of the classroom, Ms. Yoon holds up her *What's your superpower?* mug. She smiles really big, like she can't wait to get started with our class.

The pencil sharpener whirs in the back of the classroom. My mind whirs too, thinking again of all the ways I could get out of this project. Maybe I can tell Ms. Yoon that I have a really sore throat and can't speak for the next two weeks. I just have to think of a believable excuse.

"Okay, everyone," says Ms. Yoon, setting her coffee mug down on the desk. "We're going to get started!" She says this like she's about to give away ice cream cones. "Over the next week, we will be using class time to conduct research about topics that I will be assigning. These are subjects that you will debate in teams over three days, September eighteenth through the twentieth. I think you will really enjoy the process, but it will be *a lot* of work."

Lots of people's shoulders slump at the sound of "a lot of work," including mine.

"You'll also need to spend time outside of class to research," continues Ms. Yoon. "Everyone will need to consult at least five sources. These could be books, articles, videos, or reliable Internet resources."

Sean Thompson, a boy who always wears baseball hats, shoots up his hand. "Can we use Wikipedia?" he asks hopefully.

Ms. Yoon shakes her head. "No, not officially. Only as a way to find other resources. But don't worry—we will be visiting the library." She perches on the edge of her desk. "Our school librarian, Mrs. Herrick, will be giving you all kinds of tips on finding sources." She swings her legs. "The library is my favorite place in the whole world."

Okay, I can get behind that. I like libraries. Especially all of their art books.

Ms. Yoon slides off her desk and steps closer to the front row. "So, as promised, I'm going to give everyone their topics today, as well as assign groups."

Out of the corner of my eye, I see that Fiona is

soundlessly clapping her hands. She's obviously trying to kiss up to the teacher.

Ms. Yoon paces for a moment. "All of these topics are considered controversial," she says in a serious tone. "Many people are going to have strong opinions on them, which is going to make for fun and lively debates."

"If Ms. Yoon says 'fun' one more time," I whisper to Jana, "I'm going to start screaming."

"It'll be fine. Trust me," Jana whispers back.

That's easy for her to say! She just doesn't know what it's like to be not so outgoing.

"So, are you ready?" asks Ms. Yoon as if we are at a pep rally. She cups her hand behind her ear. "Can't hear you. Are you ready?" she asks in a louder voice.

"Yes!" shouts Fiona. Everyone is sort of mumbling in agreement.

"Louder!" insists Ms. Yoon. *"Are you ready?"*

This time, the thunder of stomping feet erupts from the back of the classroom. I turn around and see that it's Jacob and Lukas. They're stomping their feet and pounding their fists against their desks. The whole back row is now doing it, and soon the pounding and stomping extends through the whole classroom. Jana and I start to pound too. It's pretty fun. Like an orchestra of stomping.

Ms. Yoon makes a motion for us to stop. But she's not mad. She's smiling. "Much better, you guys. That's the spirit! So there will be groups of four assigned to each topic. And they are right here." She dramatically retracts the projector screen that was covering the whiteboard. On it are seven topics and the names of the people in each group.

Everyone leans forward, scanning the topics to see whom they're paired with. I hope I'm in a good group, and pray that Fiona is not in it.

I'm not in the THE VOTER AGE SHOULD BE LOWERED TO THIRTEEN topic. But I see that Lukas is. Nor did I get PUBLIC SCHOOLS SHOULD BAN DRESS CODES.

My eyes scan the rest of the topics. I'm not listed on any of them, until I get to the very bottom: SCHOOLS SHOULD BAN SECURITY CAMERAS.

And there's my name. I'm with Fiona, Jana, and Jacob!

Wow. I'm not sure how to feel about this. I swallow hard. I'm really happy to be with Jana. But Fiona. Awkward. And Jacob, well, that's a problem. How can I stay neutral if I have to interact with him?

Jana turns around and high-fives me. "We're in the same group! Yes!" She lowers her voice. "I'm with Jacob. This is a miracle."

Of course she said *I'm*.

But it's *we*.

We are with Jacob. And Fiona too.

Then it hits me. Yesterday, we got to pick whom we wanted to work with, and Ms. Yoon honored what we wrote. Fiona must have written down Jana's name and probably her cousin Jacob's. Jana wrote down Jacob and me. And I wrote down Jana.

Who did Jacob write down? I want to look back at him so badly. But I don't.

Ms. Yoon explains how debate is not a yelling match. It is a discussion on a topic that has been thoroughly researched. It's not personal. It's logical. She has us push our desks together in rows, forming tables of four desks each. "I want you to sit with your group," she explains, "and discuss a little bit about your topic. Just whatever comes to mind."

I don't think I've ever seen Jana move so fast. She sits in the desk directly facing Jacob's. So she can stare into his blue, blue eyes, of course.

I should sit next to Jana. I should let her have Jacob

all to herself. But I can't help myself. I sit in the desk beside him. This way I'll at least get a side view.

"Oh no! I'm surrounded," jokes Jacob. "By all girls. And my cousin."

"Ha, ha," Fiona says, and kicks his chair.

"You're lucky," smirks Jana.

"We do have the best topic," says Fiona, who sits directly across from me. "Don't you think? Way better than that cloning one."

"They all sound hard," says Jana.

"Not if we do the research," sniffs Fiona. She sits up very straight and flicks imaginary lint off her hoodie.

Jacob twirls his pencil. "I was hoping for the one about the driving age getting lowered. It'd be so awesome if I could drive next year. In a Porsche race car."

"No, it wouldn't," says Jana in mock horror.

"It'd be way too dangerous," says Fiona. Behind her glasses, her eyes grow big with worry.

Jacob crosses his heart. "I promise, if I got my license next year in eighth grade, I wouldn't run any of you over. Just your toes."

"Wow," I say, "you're so thoughtful."

And Jacob grins at me.

Even though I don't want my heart to beat extra fast, it does.

For another five minutes or so we talk about security cameras. Stuff like where we've noticed them—at malls, inside gas stations—and whether we've ever seen any security cameras at Northborough Middle School.

"I'm pretty sure there's one near the office," says Fiona.

Jacob nods. "Oh, right. That's to capture *you* on camera." He gazes at us in mock seriousness. "My cousin's such a problem child." Fiona kicks his chair again.

"I think there's one by the gym," I add.

"I don't think there's any," says Jacob, and Jana readily agrees.

Soon we launch into a huge argument about whether we need cameras. Not a serious one. But we're all debating it.

Fiona shushes us. "Quiet," she says. I forgot how bossy she is. Sure, Jana is bossy too, but in a fun way. Fiona would shush the principal. "Ms. Yoon is trying to talk." She points to the front of the classroom, where our teacher is asking us to stop our discussions so we can listen.

"Now that you've talked over your topic, here's the next step," she says. "Divide your group in half. Two of you will argue pro. Two of you will argue con. Pro means you agree with the statement. Con means you disagree with the statement. The pro team is called the *proposition* and the con team is called the *opposition*. So the con side will be everybody at desks that are on my right. And the pro side will be the opposite."

Everyone starting murmuring and trying to figure out whether they are con or pro.

"It's not that hard," states Fiona. "Jana and I are pro. And Jacob and Maddie are con."

Jacob smiles at me, and I can't help smiling shyly back. No matter how hard I try, I do still like him. It's so frustrating!

Meanwhile, Jana's face twists in confusion. "What? Are you sure? I'm pretty sure that Jacob and are on the same team."

Fiona rolls her eyes and makes a huffy noise. "No, because you're facing him. But sitting next to me. So *we* are the same team." She says *we* in a possessive way.

Jana's hand shoots up. "Ms. Yoon, can you come over here? We have a question."

Our teacher strides over and patiently explains that yes, Fiona is right. "Jacob and Maddie will be working together." And she nods at Jana and then Fiona. "You two girls will be a team. You'll be arguing *for* cameras."

"But I'm much more con," protests Jana. "Shouldn't I argue the side I believe in?"

If there was any doubt in my mind that Jana really liked Jacob, it's gone now. Not that I doubted it exactly. It's just that I was hoping she was thinking he was devolving into "very cute" versus a major crush.

To be honest, I was really hoping that she would be over it by now. That a couple of days back at school would have worn away the crush thing.

But noooooo.

Jana is my very best friend. We have to be united and respect the BFF Code. I can't ever tell her how I feel about Jacob. I don't want her to shoot dagger eyes at me like she is at Fiona right now. And I definitely don't want to lose her as my very best friend.

Ms. Yoon tours around the room, making sure that everyone understands who is on their team. "I realize you all want to be on the same side as your friend, but that won't always happen," she tells the class.

Of course, Ms. Yoon assumed that Jana wanted to be with me. And normally, if it weren't for her huge crush, that would be true.

Pfft! A balled-up piece of notebook paper hits me square on the nose. I'm about to get angry but then realize Jacob tossed it in a friendly way.

Jacob gives me his lopsided grin. "Hey," he says. "Are you ready to fight against those two? It's going to be a tough battle ahead. But I think we can do it together."

That's when it hits me (figuratively, this time): I'm on Jacob's team. Me! We're going to be working on a project together for twelve days! I know, because Ms. Yoon has just written on the board when everybody will debate. Jana, Fiona, Jacob, and I are on September eighteenth. That means for twelve days, we get to sit together and work together.

And suddenly, I'm liking this debate project a whole lot more.

Later, after class is over and Jana and I are walking down the hall, I feel guilty for being so happy to work with Jacob, so I apologize. "Sorry," I say.

"What for?" asks Jana, as we thread around a clump of eighth graders carrying band instruments.

"For getting on Jacob's, you know, team."

"Not your fault. That's Ms. Yoon's." Jana pauses. "You know, I was watching you in class. And I wonder something. Do you like Jacob?"

"What?" I vigorously shake my head. "Nooooooo. Not at all."

Jana lets out a breath. "Okay, just checking. I don't understand why we couldn't pick who we're partners with. I mean, look at me. I'm stuck with Fiona." She rolls her eyes. There's a traffic jam as we pass the birthday bulletin board. Everyone is looking to see who has a birthday in September. We don't need to look. We know.

"If it couldn't be me, I'd want it to be you," Jana says, then lowers her voice. "On Jacob's team, that is."

"Yes," I agree, speaking up because the hall is filled with the loud buzz and chatter of dozens of conversations. "I'm so happy that I can help you out." And it's not a lie. It's not a lie at all.

"I can't wait for school to be over," she says. "School is lasting forever. This day sort of sucks."

"I'm sorry," I say, and then I hug her. "Instead, think happy thoughts. Think about your birthday slumber party, which I am going to help you plan and is going to be amazing."

Suddenly Jana's face lights up. "Yes," she says. "We're a great team. It's going to be awesome."

As we high-five each other, this eighth grader clunks me in the arm with his trombone case.

"Excuse me!" Jana races after the kid before he disappears into the throng crowding the hallway. "Apologize," she demands. The kid blinks behind his smudged glasses. His long arms swing down practically to his knees. He looks like he suddenly sprouted up last week and doesn't quite know what to do with such long limbs. "Apologize for what?" He shuffles back a step, looking around as kids passing by slow down to check out the confrontation.

"For hitting my friend." Jana points at the offending trombone case. "With that."

"Oh," he says, staring at his instrument.

Jana's brows furrow. Her hands slap onto her hips.

"I'm sorry." The boy swallows hard. "Really, really sorry." He looks at me. At least, I think he does. His glasses are so fogged up, it's hard to tell. "You all right?" His voice is anxious.

"Yes," I say, trying to suppress a giggle. This boy towers over tiny Jana, yet he looks petrified. Jana has that effect on people. He turns around and hurries away.

"You're awesome," I say.

"I know," says Jana. Then we link arms and skip to fifth period.

I get home after school and say a quick hi to my mom. It's her day to work from our house—she's a librarian at Boston College, which is a pretty big commute from our town. Then I go upstairs to my room and pretty much just dance around excitedly for a half hour.

Mom calls up to ask me if I've seen Elvie, and I call down no.

I toss Mr. Monkey into the air. He's the stuffed monkey that my Grandma Anna in Philly sent me for my birthday when I was three, and I still love him.

"Oh, Mr. Monkey," I say, throwing him around. "I love you!" I kiss him and pretend to waltz with him. I throw open the blinds and gaze at the maple tree outside my window. The leaves are starting to turn bright red. "It's a glorious day," I tell Mr. Monkey.

I go downstairs to get myself a snack and pet Morty. My mother paces by the kitchen table, her forehead furrowed. I'm about to tell her how I really like her dress. How I really like everything. But I don't. I can tell my mother is upset.

Footsteps crunch along the driveway. The door opens, and Elvie slips inside the foyer. My mother glances up; she looks both relieved and angry.

"Where were you?" Mom glances at her watch.

"I had a study group," my sister says, shrugging off her backpack. "Hi, Maddie," she says. She bends down to rub Morty's neck.

"Hi," I say, but I wish I were still upstairs. Mom is not happy.

"I don't understand your school," says Mom. "You had a study group yesterday too. It's crazy! It's just the beginning of the school year—this is too much." She shakes her head.

Elvie takes off her windbreaker. "Mom, it's normal. It's AP. It's intense. And I did tell you about my study session."

"No you didn't."

"I did." Elvie hangs her coat up in the closet. "During dinner."

Mom glances at her phone. "With work right now, there's a lot going on. Maybe you did mumble something. But you need to give me meetings as a calendar item."

"Okay, I'm sorry," says Elvie, her voice tense. "I'll

do it next time. Most people would be happy that their daughter is staying after school to study."

"I am, but you just need to communicate better," says Mom.

I clear my throat. "Well, I had a really good day at school. I like all my teachers this year. In Social Studies, we got our debate topics." I tell them about how my group will be debating cameras in schools.

Mom looks thoughtful. "I'd be happy to give you some tips on finding sources. There are definitely tricks to it."

"Thanks, Mom," I say.

"She's really good at playing detective," says Elvie. "Definitely let her help you. It'll help your grade." Sometimes all Elvie cares about is grades. But right now it doesn't bother me.

Mom heads toward the kitchen. "Okay, gang. It's time to start some dinner. Your dad's going to be working late tonight on that new trial, so we'll start without him." As Mom rummages through the fridge, I say to Elvie. "How's the electric bass going?"

She puts her finger to her lips. "Later," she says. She nudges her chin toward Mom, who's pulling out a bag of kale. And I remember how my parents don't think that Elvie should tackle electric bass because of her tight schedule. Sounds like she has a secret. I know all about those.

Chapter Nine:
One Hacky Sack

On Thursday during lunch, Jana, Katie, Torielle, and I walk into the cafeteria together. We're discussing the details of Jana's slumber party, which is happening in exactly nine days. We're all really excited about the karaoke machine and the nail salon portion of the party.

Katie shakes her head. "The cafeteria is so crowded today."

"I know," says Torielle. "Most of the round tables have been claimed."

"Let's sit over there," says Jana, pointing to the table by the Fixings Bar. We all race to it, barely beating some band kids.

We all plop down and stuff our backpacks under our chairs. Out of the corner of my eye, I see Jacob and Lukas heading our way. "What if Jacob is only coming over here because he can't find a seat anywhere else?" says Jana in a worried voice. She doesn't sound like herself at all. Jana's normally so confident.

"No, there are other seats around," points out Torielle, opening a canister of stew. Steam rises into the air and it smells like carrots, cabbage, and sausage.

"It's true," says Katie, spreading out her cloth napkin before she eats as usual. "Look at all of the long tables."

But I know we're more than just a convenient seating choice, because Jacob is smiling. I freeze, because I don't want to be biting into my turkey sandwich while he's looking at me. Because unless I'm hallucinating, he's smiling right at me.

And he's heading for the open seat right next to me!

Jacob is only a few feet away when Jana gets up, grabs an empty chair from the table behind us, and somehow squeezes it in between herself and Katie.

"Jacob," she announces. "You can sit here. And Lukas can sit by Maddie."

I try not to let the disappointment show in my face. I do like Lukas just fine—he asks a lot of matter-of-fact questions and is a daredevil on his skateboard. But most of the time he likes to talk about cars. He's obsessed with them. And it's not that I don't like cars, but I don't feel like talking about them for all of lunch. Plus, I really wanted to sit next to Jacob.

As a group, we talk about a lot of things. Like how annoying raking leaves is. And how making leaf forts doesn't seem quite as much fun as it used to when we were younger. Katie talks about how her family is going to Cape Cod this weekend. It's definitely still going to be hot enough to swim. Then we get into this whole discussion about sharks. Whether anybody has actually seen one, how many great whites have been spotted off the coast of Massachusetts, and the likelihood that they would eat you.

"They just take test bites," says Lukas, who's apparently a shark guru. "They don't like human meat. They prefer sea lions."

"So they're picky, then?" I joke. The whole time, I'm sneaking little glances at Jacob.

Our eyes meet and he says, "Let's do some dares."

"I'm not eating anything gross," says Katie.

"Me either," says Torielle. "Last year some boys combined all of the ingredients on the Fixings Bar, added water, and made somebody drink it."

Lukas laughs. "That sounds awesome!"

"Okay," says Jacob. "Let's do this thing! Everyone grab some ice."

"No way." Torielle folds her arms in front of her chest. "Count me out!"

"This is a different dare," says Jacob. "Nothing to do with eating. I'll be right back."

Jacob pops up and whips over to the beverage station and back with a cup full of ice. "Okay, this is how it's going to work," says Jacob. "Everyone puts ice in their bare hands, and whoever holds it the longest, wins."

"Wins what?" asks Lukas.

"Just wins!" says Jacob.

A custodian, Mr. Stinson, walks by with a mop. "Mr. Stinson doesn't look very happy," observes Torielle.

"You guys," says Katie, "whatever you do, don't throw the ice. We shouldn't give the custodian more work."

Then Mr. Gottfried, the vice principal, walks by with his walkie-talkie crackling.

"And make sure Mr. Gottfried's out of sight before we start," says Katie.

We wait until he's safely out of view. Then Jacob tells us to put out our hands and he'll walk around and distribute ice.

He gives Jana a piece of ice first, and she gives me a look that says "This is *very* significant." As the ice slides onto her palm, she giggles.

"It tickles," she happily protests.

When it's my turn, Jacob lowers his head, so we're almost cheek-to-cheek. He smells like apples, and a little minty too.

"Thanks," I say in a normal voice. But I'm not feeling normal. This is the closest we've been since the day I spilled my pumpkin spice frappé on him.

"You're welcome," he says in a low voice and winks at me. My heart leaps. Has he winked to anybody else? No. I don't think so. Unless he just had something in his eye.

After Jacob's done distributing ice, Lukas says, "Hey, you gave me more than Jana."

"That's because he likes me more." Jana lifts her eyebrows significantly.

"It's because Jana has sweaty palms so she's already melted the ice," Torielle says, laughing.

Jana sticks out her tongue at Torielle.

Jacob heaps the most ice onto his own palm. "Okay, one, two, three, go!" he says. After thirty seconds, Lukas can't take it anymore, and he drops the ice into his drink.

"I hope you aren't planning on drinking that," says Katie, shaking her head.

"I am," says Lukas, and he takes a big gulp and crunches the ice.

"Lukas, you're such a loser," declares Jacob.

Lukas throws a balled-up napkin at Jacob's head, but Jacob ducks in time.

My hand is so numb from the cold that it aches. Katie gives up. Then Torielle. My palm is starting to throb and burn.

"I give up," I say, and dump my ice into my empty salad bowl.

Only Jana and Jacob remain. They stare at each other. They both are wincing, but neither gives up. They stay there, staring each other down until they finally declare a truce.

"We tied," says Jana happily.

"Yeah," says Jacob. "I thought for sure you were going to fold." He bites into a mini Snickers bar.

"No," says Jana. "I never give up."

I bite my lip. That's exactly what I'm afraid of.

Suddenly, Jana grabs Jacob's hacky sack and throws it to me. I catch it and throw it to Katie. The hacky sack ends up in her salad, next to a slice of tomato. Katie makes a face.

Then Vice Principal Gottfried comes up to us and says, "Girls," and then looks around and sees that we are definitely not all girls. "If you want to play hacky sack, take it outside."

"I definitely don't want to play hacky sack," says Katie, pushing away what's left of her salad.

"I do," says Jacob. And he jumps up to head outside.

Lukas throws up his hands and says, "Don't look at me. I'm still eating."

Jana leaps out of her chair. "I'm coming!"

"How about you?" asks Jacob, looking at me.

"Um, that's okay. I'll just finish my taco."

Jana gives me a grateful smile for not following her.

And the two of them leave together, one hacky sack between them.

During Social Studies, we go to the library and take a tour of the reference section. The librarian, Mrs.

Herrick, shows us how to find sources there, and how to search for reliable sources online using databases. My mom, the academic reference librarian, would be so proud.

Jacob and I spend twenty minutes doing a treasure hunt for information.

It's actually kind of fun.

Whenever we find something good, we give each other high fives. It's his idea. And then I get all paranoid and look around the library to makes sure that Jana doesn't see. I mean, Jacob and I are officially debate partners. It isn't like we shouldn't be spending time together. But the high fives involve actually touching hands, and I don't think she'd like that. But I do.

But still, it wouldn't look right if we had too much fun.

Ms. Yoon then takes us back to the classroom for the last half of class. Everyone sits with their desk smushed next to their partner's.

That means my desk touches Jacob's.

That means whenever I look up, I stare right into his eyes.

This is not fair.

Especially for someone who is trying to fall out of crush with someone.

Everyone has their three-ring binder open, and we all take notes as Ms. Yoon explains how we will do the debates.

I can hear the scratch of Jacob's pencil across his notebook paper. Knowing he's so close is *very* distracting.

Ms. Yoon wanted to make sure that opposing teams didn't sit anywhere near each other. She says that we have to keep our arguments a secret. So Jana is sitting across the room with Fiona. They seem to be whispering. I wonder about what.

"For the debate itself you will need to construct an opening statement that defines your position," explains Ms. Yoon. "In other words, it defines what you think about your topic based on the facts that you've collected. This will take five minutes of the debate. One of the debate partners will take the opening and one will take the second half of the debate, the rebuttal. We'll go over that in a minute. In the opening, you will make three points in support of your argument. Each point must include evidence to back up your claim. What do I mean? Well, facts and figures from the book or articles that you have researched. Each point can take two minutes."

Landon raises his hand. "That's it?"

Jacob smiles at me. I smile back. Right now, I don't mind having to do more work.

"No, there's more," says Ms. Yoon. "Like I said, the other partner will create a rebuttal against arguments that your opponent has made. However, a rebuttal cannot be written in advance. You need to take notes when your opponent is speaking. There will be a time limit of two minutes."

Now I shoot up my hand. "What if you read your rebuttal instead? Like, what if you can write it really quickly while your opponent is speaking?"

Ms. Yoon shakes her head. "There's no reading anything, Maddie. Not even for your opening points. You may look at note cards where you've jotted down some facts. But there is no reading. The idea is that you are so familiar with the topic, you can just talk."

I feel like sinking into a hole in the floor. Jacob and I are going to lose. There's no way I can just talk in front of everyone. I'm going to mess it up and die of embarrassment.

"What's wrong, Maddie?" whispers Jacob.

"Nothing," I lie.

Jacob's the last person I'm going tell anything to right now.

Ms. Yoon goes on to explain that we have to do a closing argument, which is like our grand finale. It sums up all of our best arguments.

Jacob leans over to me. "Maddie, you definitely don't want to read your talk from a piece of paper. At my brother's school, there was a biology teacher who always just read aloud everything she said, and it was so boring. I'm serious."

"Wow," I say, "Your brother must have hated it."

"He said it was awesome. He got to go up three levels on this game. The teacher never noticed if anyone was on their phones because she was so busy reading her lecture."

"That's crazy," I say.

Suddenly Ms. Yoon is standing right next to me. "No talking. Thank you."

My face reddens. Oh boy. Literally, oh boy. Will Jana now know my secret?

I peer across the room at her, but she just shrugs at me. She's used to getting caught talking, so for her it's no big deal.

Next Ms. Yoon explains her grading system. Something about thorough research (that part I can do), clarity of presentation (probably not happening), and how well we work together as a group.

Jacob taps me and whispers, "We can handle that."

"What?" I ask under my breath. I don't want to be caught talking in class right now.

"Working together well," he says. I smile.

Ms. Yoon continues on about how she will be looking at our presentation style and our enthusiasm, as well as the tone of our voice.

My tone will be one of fear.

"Okay, now I'm going to give you some great strategies," she continues. "While you can't write down your rebuttal, you can try to anticipate what your opponents will say. Imagine yourself as them, and think about what facts they might come up with. Then find ways to say why their argument isn't effective. That way, you can be prepared, even without writing out a speech in advance. And make sure not to share your research with the opposing side. Keep it secret," she adds.

More secrets? These days, I have enough of those.

"Decide who wants to do the opening and who

wants to do the rebuttal," says Ms. Yoon. "Go ahead and discuss it now with your partner."

I look over at Jacob. "I'll do the opening," I say, "since I'm not so hot on thinking on my feet."

"No problem, I'll do the rebuttal." He looks up at me with a lopsided grin. Then he asks, "Can I have your number?"

"Uh, sure." We exchange numbers. My heart is pounding.

"We should meet up this weekend. At the library, so we can get ahead with turning in our five sources."

"Great idea," I say. I hope my voice doesn't sound too perky.

I tell myself to calm down. He only wants to meet up with me for our Social Studies project. It's not like a date or something.

After school, as Jana and I walk to the bus, I notice one of the lockers that we pass is decorated with blue paper and little stars.

"A birthday locker!" cries Jana. "I wonder whose?"

"Probably Memito Cruz." He's a really cute sixth grader. All of the older girls love him. He's got these gray eyes with long lashes, and he struts like he's an eighth grader already. It's a Northborough Middle School tradition that on or around your birthday someone decorates your locker. Or, I should say, it's a tradition for girls to do it for their besties or sometimes for somebody they're crushing on.

Usually it's best to come to school early to do it. Some kids do it during class when nobody is around by taking a bathroom pass, but you have to check to make sure that there are no teachers or staff in sight.

As we continue to skip down the hall, Jana says to me, "Oh my gosh. I just got the best idea! We can decorate Jacob's locker for his birthday. It's this Sunday, remember?"

How could I have forgotten? That means Jacob wants me to meet up with me during his birthday weekend. I think I'm going to faint.

"Are you in?" she asks, adjusting her backpack.

"Absolutely," I agree. And I realize I might have said it a little too enthusiastically. Just hearing his name makes my heart get all thumpity. "We should do it Monday morning, early before everyone gets here," I say. "I think it's too nerve-racking to do it during break or during class on a bathroom pass."

"I totally agree. Monday morning it is! Let's go to the mall on Saturday."

"Perfect," I say, thinking, *as long as it's not the same time that Jacob wants to get together with me in the library.*

"We can buy stuff for decorating and for my slumber party," says Jana.

"It's going to be a birthday weekend!"

"Exactly," says Jana. "I feel good!"

"I feel good too!" I say.

"I feel gooder!" Jana says even louder.

"I feel extra good!" I say, and try to really mean it.

Which isn't too hard. I'm standing with my best friend. I like being a seventh grader way more than being a sixth grader when I didn't even know where the bathrooms were or how to get to the cafeteria. The sun, honey yellow, streams through a bank of windows. The sky is clear and blue. And I stand, in the middle of the hallway, with my best friend, authentically happy on a skip-through-the-hall day.

Later, when I'm home and just back from soccer practice, Mom makes me unload and load the dishwasher. Which is the grossest job ever, because the dishes piled up in the sink have fried eggs stuck to them. And Morty begs for scraps the whole time. But suddenly it doesn't seem so bad when Jacob texts me. Hey. How are you doing?

Good, I write back, And start to laugh when I think about my earlier conversation with Jana. *Actually I'm pretty sick of staring at dishes. Since I'm unloading the dishwasher.* What I didn't write was *I have to unload the dishwasher even though it's Elvie's job. She's never around.*

Then I freeze. Did Jacob really want to hear about chores?

But when I look down at my screen, I smile. Jacob wrote back, *I'm washing my parents' cars and the dog all at the same time. My dog Reilly loves the hose. He whines the minute he sees me pick it up.*

I respond, *My dad is obsessed with hoses. He bought this thing at the hardware store that keeps the hose neat when you wind it up.*

Sounds like the perfect present for Reilly lol

Do you celebrate your dog's birthday? I ask.

Yes!

Same! I write. *My dad always gets our dog treats and chew toys.*

Fifteen minutes pass as I set the dinner table and tidy up the coat area. Jacob hasn't texted back. I'm guessing—or, rather, hoping—that he's about to eat dinner like me.

Still, today seems like the best day in the whole world.

"Mom, you're the best!" I say to my mom, who's filling a water pitcher.

Dad looks up from dressing the salad. "You're in a good mood."

"Yes," I say, "That salad looks awesome."

"Thanks." He smiles. "I made my own dressing."

Mom sets the water pitcher on the table. "We're going to be eating without Elvie." She frowns.

"Let me guess," I say, settling down into my chair. "She's got a study group."

"Exactly," says Dad, sitting across from me. "Your sister's very busy these days."

"Don't worry," I pipe up. "I'll eat more than my share. We had a hard workout at practice. Seriously, you guys, thanks for making such a wonderful meal."

I breathe in the smell of the pasta sauce and the Parmesan cheese. Mmmm.

"Wow, you're in a *very* good mood," notes Dad.

"Yes," I say. "Very, very good."

Chapter Ten:
Shop Talk

A halo of light shimmers around my phone from the full moon shining through my window. I sit up in bed.

I'm staring at a new series of texts between Jacob and me. We texted some more after dinner, and then again a few minutes ago. Of course, I'm not supposed to have my phone in bed. It's a family rule. Cells turned off and charging by 9:00 p.m. But tonight feels like a good reason for an exception.

Him: *hey again*
Me: *hey*
Him: *wanna go to the library on Sunday afternoon?*

Me: *ok*
Him: *cool*
Me: ☺
Him: *night*
Me: *night*

Sighing happily, I slide down into my comforter and study the texts for the ninety-ninth time. I so want to tell someone about this. But I can't. I just can't.

Obviously trying to *not* like Jacob is not working. But liking Jacob only in my head is weird. It's equivalent to having a crush on a movie star. The truth is, I'm hoping that Jana's crush will eventually wear down.

Jana and Jacob. J&J. It's too perfect. It sounds like a clothing brand or a cool shoe store. They sound like they belong together. *Oh, stop it, Maddie*, I tell myself. *Your mind is going into nightmare mode.*

I yawn, staring up at the ceiling, where I have glow-in-the-dark stars. Only the lights have been off so long that they're not glowing any more. When I was younger, like in second grade, I used to get scared when that happened. Back then I used to be scared about a lot of things. Okay, I'm still scared. About not doing well on tests with time pressure, speaking in public, and telling Jana how I really feel about Jacob.

My phone pings. It's Jacob sending me a goodnight emoji. My finger must have accidentally turned off the silencer.

Did my parents hear? I swallow hard and hold my breath, but . . .

Nothing. They're asleep. Dad's snoring, and Mom probably has in her earplugs. I put the phone back on vibrate mode.

I glance down at my glowing screen and snuggle up next to it.

Footsteps shuffle down the hallway. Mom bangs into my still-darkened room and says in a high-pitched, very loud voice, "Maddie. What. Are. You. Doing?"

Uh oh.

Mom doesn't get angry very often, but when she does, she spews like a shaken-up soda can. Like that day Mom was freaking about Elvie. I push the covers over my head, groaning, "Mom, I'm sleeping."

"I don't think so. I heard you."

"I'm asleep," I say, curling my pillow around my head.

"Do you realize what time it is?"

Rolling over, I open one eye and glance at the clock. It's 11:18 p.m. "It's really not crazy late."

"Yes it is. You were on your phone!" Mom's eyes are all squinty, like she doesn't completely want to open them. And neither do I.

"I wasn't," I say.

She takes a deep breath. "Don't lie to me, Maddie. Things will be much easier if you just tell the truth. I'm tired and I'd like to go to bed."

So I tell her that, yes, I was texting Jana. I don't tell her the other part—that I was also texting a boy. But at this hour, I could have been texting with the Pope and Mom wouldn't care. This is not good.

Chapter Eleven:
THE PUNISHMENT

"Your parents did *what?*" asks Jana as we stand by our lockers the next morning. It's five minutes before the advisory bell rings.

"They took away my phone," I say. "Until tomorrow."

"I'm so sorry," Jana says loudly over the chattering crowd. Then she nods at Torielle and Katie, who shuffle toward us in the hallway. "Maddie got her phone taken away for a day," Jana explains to them.

"Wow, I wish my parents were that intelligent," says Torielle. "Just a day? My parents only ever take mine away for a week. Imagine a punishment that normal."

Despite how I'm feeling, Torielle makes me laugh.

"It does suck, though," says Katie, stepping over someone's fallen red water bottle being kicked around in the hallway. She gives me a hug and so do Jana and Torielle.

Torielle grabs my hands. "Maddie, you can borrow my phone during school."

"And mine," says Katie.

"And mine," says Jana, shoving a stick of gum in her mouth as she waves at a few girls we all know. The smell of cinnamon makes me blink. Walking toward our advisories, we pass a poster for a babysitting class where you can learn CPR. Now, that's something I should know, since I might need to revive myself someday from all this stress I've caused myself.

I can't borrow any of their phones—because I can't text Jacob from their phones.

My stomach clenches as I think about lunch. What if Jacob mentions something about us texting each other? And what if he tries to text me this morning? He'll think I'm blowing him off.

I blink back tears as a bunch of boys in matching high tops cut in front of me. I say to my friends, "Thanks for the phone offer. Seriously. But I'm going to be fine." Then I whisper, "Is my all face blotchy?"

"No." Torielle puts her hand on my shoulder. "You look fine."

"Don't lie. Would you let me take a photo of this"—I point to my face—"on Snappypic?" The warning bell rings, and more kids weave around us.

"Maybe a little blotchy," admits Jana as she ducks into her advisory.

"But," says Katie, "it gives your face some color."

And as dumb as it sounds, everyone being nice about my blotchy red face and saying they'll let me borrow their phones makes the not-very-good start to my day a whole lot better.

Just two days ago, we had been an all-girl table. Four friends discussing Jana's karaoke slumber party in detail, or whatever. But now we seem to be officially a boy-girl table. Actually, some of the long tables are mixed, but it's sort of accidental, where a group of guys bumps up against a group of girls.

But at the round tables, nothing is accidental. It's weird, but to other people's eyes, we probably look like the popular table—a group of girls and boys who always seem to be flirting and laughing about something.

And that's true. But we're still ourselves.

Right now the six of us are arguing about which teachers at Northborough Middle are the weirdest.

"I think Mr. Dupree, the French teacher, is the weirdest," says Torielle. "His pants are so tight and once Mason Bergeron caught him picking his nose. He just smiled and went, 'oui, la booger!'"

"I think Mrs. Gilligan wins," says Katie. "She's always licking her braces, like she likes them a little too much."

Jacob shakes her head. "I'm voting for Mrs. Haber."

"Really?" says Lukas. "Her?"

Jacob shrugs. "I don't know. I'm just being random. I really don't know the teachers well enough."

"I think she's nice and so pretty," Jana says. "And doesn't give a lot homework."

"Exactly," says Torielle. "She's normal, which at our school makes her weird."

That cracks everyone up. Then I hear Jana whispering to Jacob. "Put away your phone," she says, nodding toward Mr. Gottfried. The vice-principal's walkie-talkie crackles as usual. His eyes sweep the tables, looking for kids who are throwing food or on their phones.

Jacob's on his phone right now, looking at some game.

Jana grabs it from him. "If you're not going to put it away, I am," she says, but she's not angry. She's teasing.

I don't like the idea of her having Jacob's phone one little bit.

"Mr. Gottfried is coming!" urges Torielle. "He's five tables away and he's doing his electronics sweep."

"Put Jacob's phone in your backpack," says Katie.

Mr. Gottfried finishes his sweep of our side of the cafeteria and then heads to the opposite side.

"Okay," says Jacob. "Time to give me my phone back."

"I don't have your phone." Jana giggles. "I don't know what you're talking about."

I start to panic. What if Jana goes through his phone and sees our texts? Technically, it's okay that we've exchanged numbers. After all, we're debate partners. But she'll see that we weren't exactly just talking about Social Studies.

I move to grab it, but Jana's faster. She holds up the phone. "Oh, you mean *this* phone, right?" She waggles it.

She peers at the screen.

"Hmm, let me see. Who do you have in your contacts?"

Oh. No.

"The screen is locked," Jana says.

Phew.

Jacob grins. "Give it back."

"Tell me your passcode," says Jana.

"Yeah, right," says Jacob.

"Is it your dog's name?" Jana says. "Actually, I don't even need to type to get into your phone."

"How?" asks Jacob, curious.

"Talent," says Jana. "It's this new app where you just think your thoughts and your phone texts for you."

"Really?" ask Lukas.

"Yeah, it's called mind reader." Jana giggles again.

"I want that," says Torielle, and I'm smiling so hard the peas in my mouth are about to roll out and down the table. I'm relieved. There's no way that Jana is going to be able to see my texts to Jacob.

"Where can you get the mind reader?" asks Lukas in a serious voice.

"She's kidding, you guys," says Torielle. I burst out laughing and then I have to hold it in because I'm kind of snorting and some of the chocolate milk I just drank is tickling my nose. I know it's just nerves.

The guys crack up, mostly at me sounding like a goose. Jana, Torielle, and Katie are laughing too.

"You guys," says Lukas, putting down a slice of pizza. "I thought that the mind-reader app was real, and I really, really wanted it."

"What if I told you this fork is a mind reader?" I say.

Lukas pushes back his chair. "I'd say awesome."

"Has anyone noticed how we're always talking about utensils at this table?" points out Jacob.

"Yes," says Torielle. "But not ordinary utensils. Sporks and mind readers."

We all crack up some more.

During Social Studies, Ms. Yoon hands out debate forms that we have to fill out and turn in for a grade, then gives us the rest of class to work with our partners. There's an opening statement and a rebuttal form, and then a form for each of us to list our five sources.

"It's a lot," I say, looking at the two forms. I start reading the opening statement worksheet aloud. "The opening has to have a hook, such as a statistic or quote, that grabs the audience. You have to clearly define your position in the debate, and then provide a minimum of three arguments supporting your position, backed up by facts or statistics." I put down the sheet. "Plus, there's the rebuttal sheet. And the bibliography info."

"Phew," says Jacob.

I shake my head. "I only found two sources at the school library the other day."

"Don't worry. We'll find what we need on Sunday."

"Yeah," I say, and I can't help grinning. As if I'd forgotten we were planning on meeting at the public library Sunday afternoon!

"By the way, there's something I wanted to let you know," I say. "I got my phone taken away. So I won't be able to respond to texts until tomorrow morning."

"Are your parents really strict?" he asks.

"Sort of." I shrug, embarrassed.

"Mine too." He gives me his lopsided grin.

"So you understand?"

"Oh yeah," says Jacob.

Then I see Jana heading right toward us like she has some sort of radar. On the other side of the room, Fiona sits at her desk, furiously scribbling something into her notebook, but she keeps staring at me too, like she knows something is happening.

My face gets warm.

Jacob looks up at Jana, grinning. "Well, if it isn't the enemy."

Jana grins back at Jacob. "Well, if it isn't the con side."

He gives her a thumbs-up. "Yup, that's us. The cons." He glances over at me like we're two bank robbers who are about to pull off a heist or something.

"What's going on?" I say, keeping my voice casual.

"I want to talk about something," she says to me.

"Right now?"

She nods. "Let's go over by the pencil sharpener."

Together we shuffle over to the sharpener, and my heart starts thumping. "So, what's up?" I ask.

"I think you should do the rebuttal and go against me," Jana says.

"The rebuttal? No way. I was planning on doing the opener. You have to make up the rebuttal on the spot. I mean, Ms. Yoon says you can anticipate some stuff. But still, no. Just no."

Jana sighs heavily. "Do you really want to go right after Fiona? She's on the debate team. Just like Jacob." She points her chin over in his direction.

"No, I don't want to go after Ms. Debate herself. I actually don't want to go at all. You know that."

"Look, I don't want to go after Jacob." Jana leans in closer to me. "We can go up against each other and it'll be just fine. We both know we love each other. Let Jacob go up against Fiona, his cousin. It'll be better. They're both debate people anyway."

"Well, I don't know." I look back at Jacob, wondering what he'll think. "I might get nervous, since we're friends."

"So? You're going to get nervous anyway. Do it for me. Please." She clasps her hands together. "Pretty please with whipped cream, rainbow sprinkles, and a cherry on top?"

"Oh, all right." I sigh. "I'll do it. How can I say no to my best friend?"

Jana throws her arms around me. "You're the best, seriously."

"Sure," I say, thinking, *I'm not the best—I'm excited about meeting up with Jacob at the library, even though you have a crush on him.* No, I'm not really the best friend at all.

"What did Jana want?" asks Jacob when I slide back into my chair.

I explain how she wants me to do the rebuttal.

"I'm cool with that," he says. "I'm actually happy to take on Fiona. I know her well, so I'll be able to attack. It'll be just like Christmas morning at Grandma's!" He puts up his arms like claws and makes a hissing sound.

I giggle.

"We're going to devour the pro team. They're in big trouble," says Jacob.

I can't bear to tell him that it's probably the opposite. We're the team that's in big trouble. All because of me.

Chapter Twelve:
Uh Oh!

It's Saturday morning, I have my phone back, and I just got a text from Jacob! My heart drums happily. It's rainy outside, dreary and still sort of dark, but I don't care.

I quickly text him back, glancing toward the front door. I'm parked on the couch in the living room, on the lookout for Jana. We're planning on riding bikes to the mall soon. Morty sits on the couch next to me, and I'm rubbing his belly.

Jacob is texting about this song, "Lemon Ginger Afternoon," by this group called the Ramon Project. *You've got to listen to it. It will blow your mind. Seriously. It's heavy metal mixed with hip-hop. But then there's some classical. And random sounds. Like a lawn mower and a baby crying.*

I go to the link he sends. The song is like nothing I've ever heard. (Usually I just listen to pop music.) Just when it gets to be really out-of-control guitar/screaming/heavy-metal sounding, it morphs into what sounds like a violin concerto, and then it goes all hip-hop.

It's really wild, I text Jacob. *In a good way. You can't even say what it is.*

Exactly. You can't just lump it into some category.

Like people.

Yup ☺

Altho right now I'm pretty much a professional dog scratcher, I write. I look up. Jana should be showing up at any moment.

When the front door opens, I'll stuff my phone under a cushion and leap into the kitchen so Jana won't see that I've been texting Jacob. My stomach tightens. I should stop texting him, but I don't want to.

Another ping. I glance down. Jacob has texted, *Does 1:00 tomorrow at the library work?*

Perfect, I text back.

Also it's my birthday tomorrow.

I can't text back, "I knew that," since it would seem like I'm trying to memorize his life. But I'm excited that he wants to see me on his actual birthday! Instead I text, *Is going to the library your birthday present? ha ha.*

My grandparents took me out to dinner last night. And I'm having friends spend the night tonight. So I'm gonna milk this birthday thing all weekend.

Birthday week? I text back.

Birthday month! he writes.

I smile and send back the birthday cake emoji.

Since Jana will be here any second, I quickly put my cell on vibrate.

Footsteps thud from the hallway. Morty starts barking. Jana's here!

I toss the phone into the sofa pillows, and I bolt up to race toward the kitchen and away from my phone.

But I don't make it there. I'm standing a few feet from the couch, and I freeze as Jana charges into the living room with bright red cheeks. She looks angry. I swallow hard. Morty barks.

"So you know?" I say.

Yeah, it's definitely too late for secrets now.

"Yeah, and I can't believe it," says Jana, her hands on her hips. "Fiona told me."

Fiona, his cousin. Of course, Jacob told her that we were meeting at the library.

"I'm sorry. Jana, I'm so sorry, seriously."

"What do you mean? It's not your fault," she says.

"I know it's not my fault. It just happened," I say, my heart pounding. "It's just about taste, I guess."

"Taste? What are you talking about?" Jana scrunches her forehead in confusion.

"What are *you* talking about?" I say, gulping.

She pulls out a sheet of paper out of her purse. "For the PTA Haunted House. We're not on the same schedule. At all. Even though I signed up to work with you! I'll be working with Fiona instead. I don't know how it happened."

"Oh, that. Yeah. That's okay—it's just one day." I can feel relief washing over me.

Jana squints her eyes. "Wait a minute. What were *you* talking about? You weren't talking about schedules. You said 'it just happened,' and something about taste."

"Oh, I . . . I was just talking about how nobody can figure out why somebody like Fiona would have a cousin with as much good taste as Jacob."

Jana looks at me strangely. "Okay, whatever." She wipes her forehead as if it's hot in the room. "You have such a serious look on your face."

"It's the debate. I've been thinking about it a lot."

Morty starts barking at a squirrel outside until I shush him.

Uh oh. My phone peeks out from under the sofa cushion.

I reach back with my fingertips to poke it further back. I pray that the pillow doesn't flop backwards, exposing my phone with Jacob's text probably on the screen.

The pillow stays in place. Justice reigns in the universe.

"Ready to do some shopping?" asks Jana. "Afterward, we can get ready for our soccer game together."

"Yes," I say, "most definitely."

Chapter Thirteen: SHOP 'TIL WE DROP

At the mall, Jana and I stand in front of the cologne hut. Jana sprays a tester bottle, and the air smells like lemons and watermelon. The mall is packed, since it's rainy today.

"We're going to spray Jacob's locker with cologne?" I ask.

Jana giggles. "Well, it is a very manly scent."

I plug my nose. "Please, no. Eww."

She grabs something called Watermelon Water, and I laugh. "Well, if Jacob likes watermelons a lot, then it's perfect!"

The saleswoman notices us, and her smile becomes taut. She sticks her hands into her apron pocket. "How can I help you girls today?" she asks, her voice polite but tinged with an edge.

"Um, my friend is looking for something for her . . . friend . . . who is a boy," I say.

Jana elbows me and turns red.

Out of the corner of my eye, I see a guy leaning against the counter. He looks like Jacob. The same reddish-brown hair. My insides flip-flop. Oh no. The guy turns around, and he's got zits all over his face and a weird mustache.

So not Jacob. Phew.

"Well," says the saleswoman. "Let me know if you have any questions." She turns to help a middle-aged woman wearing a raincoat that looks like a trench coat from a spy novel.

Jana is spritzing and pumping all of the bottles on the counter. Soon we'll both smell like every scent combined into one. "We should go," I say. "We don't have a ton of time before we have to get ready for soccer."

"There are still some scents to try!" Jana says. "But okay, fine. I'll go." She grabs a couple of free samples and zips them into the pocket of my backpack.

We thread around packs of people holding various shopping bags and head toward the arts and crafts store. I pop in my earbuds and listen to "Lemon Ginger Afternoon" and just start grinning.

Meanwhile, Jana is ticking off a list on her fingers. She taps me on the shoulder. "You're not listening."

"Sorry," I say. "This song's just so freaking awesome." I hand Jana my headphones and she listens, wrinkling her face in distaste. She yanks off the buds and hands them back. "Since when do you listen to heavy metal?" I can tell she's shocked. Jana is a total pop music girl.

"It's not really heavy metal," I protest.

Jana shakes her head. "Well, no thank you."

"It's also classical and hip-hop and—"

"I believe you. Where did you even find that song, anyway?"

My heart speeds up. "I, um . . . I came across it on Spotify."

Jana shrugs. "Whatever. Anyway, we better get onto shopping essentials. This is what we need to decorate Jacob's locker for his birthday: wrapping paper, ribbons, balloons, candy, sticky notes, and happy birthday banner."

"That all sounds good," I say as we maneuver around a new electric car on display in the center court. It's part of some mall giveaway, and there's actually a small line to buy raffle tickets.

When we get to the arts and crafts store, we go straight to the wrapping paper area. Jana picks out some red paper, but I suggest we get blue instead, since Jacob is always wearing blue shirts. It's probably his favorite color. It matches his amazing eyes too—but I don't say that part aloud.

Next, Jana starts to grab a happy birthday banner, but I shake my head. "The foam letters will look better," I say. "That way, we can spell out his name." Then I grab a bunch of foam sticker soccer balls. "Jacob will love these."

"Brilliant idea," says Jana, looping her arm through mine.

After we purchase everything, we head to the candy store to pick up some treats—mini Snickers—to tape to the front of his locker. On our way, we pass by a jewelry store, and Jana slows down. She's staring at a necklace that's made of beads that look like little soccer balls. I make a note to come back later and check it out. I have a feeling it would be the perfect birthday present for Jana.

After the candy store, we go to a beauty discount

place to pick out nail polish, cotton balls, and nail polish remover for Jana's slumber party.

"We should play spin the bottle," I say as we walk down the aisle to the nail polish section.

Jana's eyes widen in surprise. "Are you kidding? My mom would kill me."

"It's not what you think. I'm talking about a game I read about online—it's a nail polish game. You have a spinner and then whatever color you land on, you have to paint your nails that color. The game's over when everyone's nails are painted."

"Oh, I love it! Let's do it," says Jana. "But where do we get the spinner?"

"We can just use the spinner from my old Hi Ho! Cherry-O game," I say. "I'll cover over the game box."

Jana hugs me. "Oh, you are so crafty and artsy. Thank you thank you thank you! We're going to have so much fun."

We spend the next fifteen minutes debating colors, then pay for everything and decide to go to the food court for a snack. When Jana says she has to go to the bathroom, I tell her to meet me in front of our favorite ice cream place because I forgot that I needed to pick up a roll of Scotch tape for my mom.

This is such a lie. Instead, I race to the jewelry store and buy the soccer ball necklace, because it really is absolutely perfect for Jana. It's a little expensive, but my Nana down in Virginia gave me a ton of birthday money this summer (my birthday is July twenty-second), and I hadn't spent a lot of it. I spot this adorable heart key chain on sale, and I buy it too. Then I rush back to meet Jana at the ice cream place.

I'm hurrying past the south entrance when I pass a bunch of guys eating soft pretzels. Then I realize they aren't just any bunch of guys. It's Jacob with a group of his friends. Some I recognize. Some I don't.

Do they see me? I hope not!

I can feel my ears turn pink as I hunker down into my hoodie.

"Hey, is that Maddie?" I can hear Jacob say.

"That definitely is," yells Lukas.

"Hi," I say, stopping. I really don't have a choice.

"Hey, Maddie," says Jacob. "Want some pretzels?" He holds up a bag. "We have lots."

They smell good, but I really don't have time. I look both ways for Jana. "Um, that's okay."

"Do you have a soccer game this afternoon?" he

asks, while his friends huddle, looking at something on one of their phones.

"Yup," I say.

"Me too." Jacob looks back at his friends. They're still huddling, but they keep on looking over at us. I'm not quite sure what they're expecting to happen.

"Maybe I'll see you," I say lamely.

"Yeah. That'd be cool."

"Well, I've got to meet a friend. So I better go." I wave goodbye.

"All right, 'bye. See you later," calls out Jacob.

As I start to walk away, his friends nudge him with their elbows.

I can feel myself blushing. They obviously know he's meeting me at the library tomorrow afternoon, on his actual birthday.

A minute later, I'm startled when Jana is right in front of me. "Was that Jacob?" she asks. "I thought I saw him and his friends talking to you."

"Um, yeah." Oops.

"Why didn't you text me to come?" Her eyes look murderous.

"There wasn't time. Anyway, look at the bags you're carrying!" I point to her see-through bags from the arts and crafts store. "Full of decorations for Jacob's locker. It would ruin the surprise."

"You're right," says Jana. She sighs. "What would I do without you?"

I smile, but my heart sinks because I had to tell another lie. My fingers clamp tightly onto the bag with Jana's birthday presents inside. *I did what I had to*, I tell myself.

Chapter Fourteen:
Game On

A few hours later, I'm squeezing in for the group hug. Our soccer team just won a game against a really strong squad from Worcester. Luckily, the rain from this morning cleared up—the sky is pure blue, and it's a perfect September Saturday.

"Go, Cheetahs!" we shout, our arms linked around each other.

Coach Willmert claps her hands. "Okay, Cheetahs! You played tough out there. Let's keep it up. Remember to keep on hydrating and to rest up this weekend. See you at practice on Tuesday. Oh, and I'll be sending you a message about the tournament coming up in October." She grabs her clipboard, where she keeps all of our stats. "Just remember to keep communicating with each other on the field. There were some missed opportunities. We won and I'm proud of that, but I think there were moments where you weren't connecting. Just keep talking. It's vital."

We break apart and everyone heads over to the line, where parents are folding up their camping chairs. Somewhere a lawnmower roars in the distance.

Jana wipes the back of her hand across her forehead. "I'm dead," she says, picking up a water bottle. She chugs what is left, which isn't a lot.

"You should be," I say. "You were so awesome."

Everyone's busy packing up their soccer bags. Girls from our team pass by, high-fiving Jana.

"Five goals!" shouts Brianna Walton, jogging backwards. "You're amazing."

"It's true," I gush.

"Thanks," says Jana, her face lit up with a smile.

"They tried to shut you down, but they couldn't," I say as we head toward Jana's parents, who are putting away the team's portable shade structure. Mrs. Patel is the team manager.

"That was a great game," Jana says, stuffing her

water bottle into her soccer backpack. "You were good, too, Maddie."

"Thanks," I say, but I know it's not exactly true. I only played at the end of each half for about six minutes, when it was clear that we were up by a strong lead. "I didn't let the other team score or anything."

"Nope, you held steady." Jana blocks a soccer ball zooming over from someone practicing on the field before it hits a grandpa packing up a chair.

Holding steady. It doesn't sound very impressive. More like, *Oh, congrats. You weren't bad. You were mediocre and didn't suck.* But I know Jana means well. She's always encouraging me.

My parents didn't come to the game because Elvie's chamber group had a concert. Mom and Dad never miss a concert. Anyway, there's a ton of soccer games during the season. They'll go to plenty of them. Plus, they only get to watch me play on the field for a dozen minutes anyway.

So this afternoon, Mr. and Mrs. Patel will drive me home.

"That was a great game, girls," says Mr. Patel, zipping up his windbreaker. "You didn't relent." He claps his hands together. "Ready to head home?"

Jana gazes past him to the field on the other side of ours. Her mouth suddenly drops open. "Dad, I'm not quite ready to leave."

He looks around. Mrs. Patel stands engrossed in a conversation with another soccer mom. Gus, the Patels' dog, sits next to her. "That makes two of you. Your mom hasn't even noticed that another team is now on the field." He glances at his phone. "How much more time do you need?"

Jana shrugs. "Twenty minutes."

"Twenty minutes? Are you going to get a new hairstyle? Paint your nails?"

"Dad, that's so sexist." Jana swings her backpack. "Really." Her eyes glue onto the adjacent field. "A friend is playing and I want to support him."

I look at Jana in confusion. "Who?" I ask. Jana nudges me with her elbow. Maybe Jana has a new crush. I start to feel hopeful.

"Yes, who? And a 'him'? A boy?" Mr. Patel looks both amused and concerned.

"A friend, Dad. I'm sure you have stuff to do on your phone, right?" Mr. Patel works for an engineering firm. Jana is never quite sure what he does, but she says that there are a lot of buildings in downtown Boston that will weather any storm because of him.

"Fine," Mr. Patel says. "Fifteen minutes. I'm sure your mom won't notice." He pauses. "So, Maddie—" Mr. Patel nods over at the adjacent field "—is this boy a friend of yours too?"

I peer at the field and try to figure out who Jana means. Then my eyes stop at the goal—and, specifically, who's in the goal.

Jacob.

"Yes," I say. "I know him. He's a friend." I emphasize the word friend.

"Okay, a friend of both of yours. Got it." Mr. Patel unfolds his chair to sit down on it again. "Well, go for it. Cheer him on. But take some energy bars with you, please. You need some protein." He pulls a couple of them out of a cooler. "They're chocolate."

"Thanks, Mr. Patel," I say.

Jana gives him a thumbs-up, and she tears over to the sidelines of the other field. She starts immediately screaming and yelling for the Rattlers, Jacob's team.

Not that they need any help. They're completely dominating the field.

The other team, the Lightning Bolts, are in very orange uniforms and look like they are wearing themselves down on attacks against the Rattlers' rock-solid back line. They charge down the field in a fury, but they can't get anything in the goal. Jana and I both unwrap our PowerBars.

"What's the score?" Jana asks a dad sitting in a chair next to his toddler, who's playing with a truck.

"Two to zero, the Rattlers." The dad says this in a mopey way, which lets me know he's a Lightning Bolts dad.

Suddenly someone from the Lightning Bolts' midfield breaks free of the Rattlers' defense and drills the ball within shooting distance of the net. The forward shoots, and the ball flies up high toward the far left of the net.

Jacob makes a diving save.

The Lightning Bolts' supporters groan.

"Their goalie is crazy good," says a woman in a plaid sweater. She's talking about Jacob! Both Jana and I nod in agreement, and my chest swells with pride. It's ridiculous, I know. Still, I feel like shouting, *He's my debate partner and we've been texting and we're meeting at the library tomorrow on his birthday!* but

I don't. I take a bite of the PowerBar. It's really good—chocolaty and marshmallowy.

Jana nudges me. "See, I told you Jacob's a wall."

"Yeah." I wipe my mouth with the back of my hand.

Jana and I cheer like crazy. "Way to go, Jacob!"

In the net, Jacob kind of nods at us.

Our cheering section also catches the eye of a pretty woman with bright blue eyes and short, dark-ish, reddish hair. She's sitting in a chair just a few feet away. I recognize her from the Friendly Bean—she's Mrs. Matthews, Jacob's mom! She smiles at me and does a little wave.

Oh no. She's walking over to talk to me.

"It's so nice to see you here," she says, suddenly standing right next to me and Jana.

"We know Jacob from school." I emphasize the school part.

"So we're his cheering section," explains Jana.

"That's great," Mrs. Matthews says with a smile. She nods at our cleats and uniform. "So I see you both play soccer too. Did you just finish up a game?"

"Yes," says Jana. "We play for the Cheetahs. Girls thirteen and under."

"We won," I explain, "mostly because of her." I tap

Jana's sleeve. "So we're just taking a break. And"—I hold up the PowerBar—"rewarding ourselves."

Mrs. Matthews studies me. She has a wry smile on her face. "You girls should reward yourself with something special at the Friendly Bean afterward. It's so close by. Just make sure that you don't spill on anyone."

"Uh, okay," says Jana, raising her eyebrows in confusion. "We'll be careful."

"Yeah," I say, tugging Jana's arm, before Mrs. Matthews says something that will really get me in trouble. "Oh, shoot. We've got to go." I point my thumb to the other field. "Her dad said we needed to go back."

"But—" protests Jana.

"Nice to meet you, Mrs. Matthews," I say.

"'See you girls later. Come by to cheer for the Rattlers any time."

Jana shoots me a look. "What was that about? Am I crazy or was that just plain weird?" She covers her mouth to stifle a laugh.

"It was," I admit. But not for the reason Jana thinks.

"I mean. Sure. Who wouldn't want something at the Friendly Bean? But why does she think we'll spill on somebody? It's not like we have giant stains on our uniforms." Jana studies my face. "Actually, come to think of it, Maddie, you do have a little bit of chocolate on your chin." She brushes it off with her thumb.

"Thanks," I say, as we head toward Mr. and Mrs. Patel.

"But why did you want to leave so badly?"

"Well," I say, shrugging. "I just wanted to save us from any more weirdness."

"Jacob's mom could be an alien with green skin from the planet Zebok and I wouldn't care," says Jana.

"That would make Jacob an alien," I say.

"But a very cute one."

True, I think.

"Really, though. Why the hurry?" Jana presses.

"Just trying to be time conscious. Your dad said fifteen minutes," I protest. "I just want to make it easier on him."

Jana shakes her head. "I don't know, Maddie. I think maybe you're afraid of boys or something. We're going to have to work on this. I think we're going to have to find you a crush of your very own."

"That'd be a good idea," I say. And then inwardly sigh.

Chapter Fifteen:
A BOY AND BOOKS

I drag Mr. Mouse, my stuffed animal who used to be pinker than Torielle's lip gloss but is the color of old bubble gum, to look out the window. This morning the clouds lie low and heavy, and there's a chill in the air. But I feel so excited. This afternoon, I'm meeting Jacob in the library! There's no way I can sleep in.

It's only seven in the morning, and I'm supposed to meet Jacob at 1:00 p.m., so that means I've got to wait six entire hours. I'm not really sure what I'm going to do with myself. Well, actually I do have some idea. I listen to "Lemon Ginger Afternoon" a few times. For about an hour, I make Jacob a birthday card. On the cover I draw a bunch of soccer balls. On the inside, I write *Happy Birthday, Jacob! From Maddie.* Then I change my outfit about five times. Not something I normally do. That's more like a Torielle or a Jana thing.

I try on a knit dress with galaxies on it, but decide it looks too geeky. I put on a romper, but just no. Then I put on a soccer shirt and warm-up pants, and I realize I look like I just walked off the playing field. I finally settle on an open-shoulder long-sleeve light denim t-shirt, leggings, and white tennis shoes.

After I decide on my Jacob outfit, Mom keeps me plenty busy. Laundry. Then I have to tidy up the family room and kitchen while Elvie vacuums. And Morty sniffs around, hoping to get a treat. My sister actually cleans without claiming she has some important AP project to do. I'm pretty surprised.

We catch up for a moment, and I ask her what's happening with the electric bass stuff. "It's going great," she tells me. Her voice sounds excited. "Since I play upright, there's a lot of stuff I already know. I'm progressing fast."

"But you don't even have an electric," I say, confused.

"That doesn't mean I can't practice the fingerings.

Correct technique's so important. It minimizes fatigue and injury."

"Are you afraid that when you get an actual bass, you'll mess up?"

"Do you mean am I afraid I'll embarrass myself?" She shrugs. "Sure. I probably will. But it's not about mistakes. It's what you learn from them."

"Wow," I say. "You sound like one of Mom's self-help books."

Elvie pokes me. "How would you know? Have you been reading them?"

I can feel my face warm. "Maybe."

"Me too," she says. "Sometimes when I get stuck, I'll just randomly open one of Mom's books and see if there's some good advice there for me. And guess what? Sometimes it helps."

Later, I grin thinking about Elvie thumbing through Mom's books, just like me. I guess I always thought she had everything together. That she didn't need any extra help.

The rest of the morning crawls, but soon enough it's lunchtime and then at twelve forty-five I'm actually riding my bike to the public library.

I'm locking up my bike when I see Jacob on the

other side of the parking lot. He's on foot and waves to me.

"Hi there," I say, as he comes over to the bike rack. Today, he's wearing a gray-and-blue striped long-sleeved t-shirt, jeans, and gray Chuck Taylors. Like me, he's wearing a backpack. I'm glad I occasionally forget how cute he is. Otherwise, I probably couldn't speak to him at all.

I turn my combination so the lock will be secure. "Oh, and happy birthday!" I pull the card I made out of my backpack and hand it to him. "This is for you."

"Thanks," he says. He studies the mini Snickers taped to the front of the card. "These are my favorite."

"I know. They're really good. Plus, I've seen you eating them at lunch."

"You're an awesome artist," he says, reading the inside of the card, where I drew a close-up of a foot kicking a ball.

My face gets hot. We walk up the steps of the library together, and our hands brush so close they almost touch.

Jacob pauses to hold the door open for a woman with a stroller. "Why, thank you," says the woman, smiling at Jacob.

We walk past the circulation desk, where there's a line of people waiting to check out books.

"So where should we go?" I say.

"I guess where there's lot of books."

"Ha, ha." A little boy races past while his father, laden with an armful of picture books, pursues him.

"We can sit over near the newspaper area," says Jacob, nodding toward the center of the library. "There are lots of tables over there."

We find an empty table near the racks of newspapers from around New England and even the rest of the world. Behind the newspapers, reference books fill the shelves.

"I think we're in the right place," I say, pointing to the nearby reference desk. Two librarians stand behind the desk, helping patrons with questions. There's a stack of little pieces of paper and small yellow pencils by them and by the computers around the room.

"I always wondered about those pencils," I say. "Why are they are always yellow? And so little? And how are they always sharp, and why don't they have erasers? And why don't you see those pencils anywhere else in the universe?"

"You ask very bold, life-shattering questions, my Padawan," jokes Jacob. "I think it's the way of the Force."

"Or maybe there's some invisible librarian whose job is just to sharpen little yellow pencils!"

"Maybe. Or maybe they get a good deal on little pencils?" suggests Jacob. He squints like he's thinking hard. "You know, I think they get the same deal at miniature golf places. They have small pencils there too."

"I think it's a conspiracy. Librarians and miniature golf places are all working together."

"Definitely."

"So, I feel like I should sing you 'Happy Birthday' or something," I say. "But you don't want me to—I can't carry a tune." I laugh.

Jacob laughs too, and says, "I mostly celebrated my birthday yesterday. You saw my friends and me at the mall yesterday before soccer, and then my friends spent the night last night."

"Oh yeah," I say casually, like I barely remember. Ha! I pull my binder out of my backpack. "Sorry I couldn't talk yesterday at the mall. I had this thing with a friend."

"It's all okay. I get it." He pauses. "Thank you for coming to watch me play goalie."

"Oh, sure," I say, trying to keep my voice breezy. "It was right after our soccer game. So, should we start some actual work?"

"I don't know . . . maybe we can debate the miniature pencil conspiracy theory instead." We both laugh.

Over the next couple of hours, we fill out our opening statement and rebuttal sheets. And find a lot more sources. In the opening statement, we remember to use persuasive language, and for the rebuttal section, we brainstorm what Jana's and Fiona's arguments might be, so we can come up with good counterarguments.

I glance at my phone and realize I have to be home in forty minutes. How did time evaporate like that?

I tap the chart with my pencil. "So, take a look at this sentence in the rebuttal section. Ms. Yoon wants us to use a transition word. Do you think this works? I used 'however' instead of 'but.'"

"I can't read it upside down," says Jacob. "I really think I need to sit right next to you."

I don't object. Jacob scootches his chair over by me.

Then, together, side by side, we finish up the rest of the rebuttal section.

I thought sitting across from Jacob was a big deal.

Sitting side by side is a bigger deal.

I'm sort of having a little bit of trouble concentrating. But it's a good kind of trouble.

Chapter Sixteen:

Operation Decoration

It's Monday morning, and Jana is taping wrapping paper to Jacob's locker.

"It definitely needs a ribbon," I say. "That way the locker will look like a giant present."

"You expect me to get a ribbon straight?" asks Jana.

"I'll do it," I say cheerfully. The hallways are still quiet since we arrived at school early, but an occasional teacher passes by, slowing down to smile and watch our progress.

I use a ruler to keep the ribbon straight, tape it, and then put a giant bow where the lines of ribbon intersect.

"That looks really good," says Jana. "I'm glad I've got you as my secret weapon."

"You're welcome."

After I peel off the letters to spell *Happy Birthday Jacob,* I press the soccer ball foam stickers to the front of his locker. Meanwhile, Jana tapes up the mini Snickers bars we bought at the mall.

"We better hurry," she says, nodding at some kids drifting into school. "What if he catches us?"

"Don't worry, I'm done." I stand back and admire my work.

"Oh, we almost forgot the balloons." Jana attaches the three silvery-blue helium ones that all say Happy Birthday. She claps her hands. "It looks soooooo good."

"It does!" I say.

"Now the final touch." Jana pulls a neatly folded-up piece of paper out of her backpack. It's a note that says *Enjoy! Xx Your Secret Crush.* She drew a little soccer ball underneath. "I think he'll figure out that this"—she waggles her fingers over the locker like she's a magician—"is all from me." Then she slips the note into the locker through one of the vents.

"Yes," I say. "I'm sure he will." Jana grins from ear to ear. She looks so happy. And I want her to be happy.

But I can't help but feel jealous. After all, the locker decorations weren't all Jana. Not at all. So I also kind of hope her secret stays that way—a secret.

"Guess what?" calls out Jacob. He's approaching our lunch table. Everyone else is already sitting down. We're at our usual space near the Fixings Bar. "Someone decorated my locker!" says Jacob. "That's why I'm late."

Jana and I both try to look innocent.

"Oh really?" Jana opens her thermos of soup, and the scent of lentils wafts into the air.

"Yup." He digs into his pockets and throws a bunch of mini Snickers bars onto the table. "They gave me all of these. And left me a mysterious note."

Katie and Torielle give Jana and me conspiratorial looks. They know all about Operation Decorate Jacob's Locker.

Lukas reaches across the table and grabs all of the Snickers.

"You better share, Mr. Greedy," says Jacob.

"I am sharing," says Lukas. He unwraps a bar and pops it into his mouth, swallows, then adds, "With myself."

Jana giggles. "You're crazy, Lukas."

Jacob lunges and swipes a bunch away from Lukas. "Here," he says, dropping one beside Torielle's lunch bag. "One for you."

Stalking up behind Jana, he tosses a Snickers into her lap. "Thanks!" she squeals, like somehow this particular bar is extra special and was selected just for her.

Then he tosses two more. One lands by my lunch sack and one by Katie's.

"Are you going to keep any for yourself?" I ask.

"Don't worry." Jacob rubs his belly. "I've already had plenty."

"So who decorated your locker?" Lukas takes a bite into another bar and chews thoughtfully. "'Cause I can tell you it wasn't me."

"I don't know for sure," says Jacob. He plops down across from me and next to Jana. "But I have a good idea who it could be. It's someone who plays soccer."

Jana's eyes glimmer.

"And someone who's good at art," continues Jacob.

Jana bites her lip. She's definitely not good at art.

I am, though.

"And someone who knows I like mini Snickers." He pulls out his lunch and then stuffs his backpack under his chair. Then he taps his chin. "Hmmm, to the mysterious person who wants to keep themselves a secret: thank you." He gives a thumbs-up. "Mysterious person, you did an awesome job."

I so badly want to say *You're welcome*. Instead I just gaze down at my Snickers and try not to smile.

On our way to Social Studies, Jana is not happy. Kids mob the hallways and elbows and backpacks bang into our sides.

"I can't believe he couldn't figure out that note was from me," she moans. "It was in *my* handwriting."

"Maybe you should have signed it with a J or something? Well, next time."

"Next time?" Jana stops to drink from the water fountain. The fountain doesn't work. She kicks it. "Next time is a whole year from now! I can't wait for that!"

Especially since you will have changed crushes two dozen times by then, I want to say. But I don't. I know she's feeling awful. And I feel bad that she's feeling bad. However, I also feel happy inside. Jacob thought the locker decoration was from me!

In Social Studies, Jacob and I work together on a

debate vocabulary sheet. Basically, Ms. Yoon has us look up the terms, like *resolution* and *assertion*, and write them out on a worksheet that she passed out. Jacob is pretty flirty the whole time, kicking my foot under the desk. The task of looking up words flies by.

Afterwards, I have Science with Torielle. She sits across from me.

"I don't see Mr. Gibson," Torielle says. The bell has rung, but a bunch of kids are out of their seats chatting. Some are even sitting on top of the back counter.

"He's not here. Maybe he's out sick," I say hopefully. "Maybe we have a sub."

"I think he had to visit the men's 'facilities.'" Torielle lowers her voice and makes quotes in the air with her fingers.

"How do you know? Did you see him take a bathroom pass?" I joke.

"I can sense things," Torielle smiles mysteriously.

"So you're psychic?"

She pinches her fingers. "Just a little," she jokes.

Soon enough, Mr. Gibson waltzes back into the room and says, "Sorry, folks. I had an emergency call." He fingers his mustache, and as he walks he's saying, "Just because I was not here doesn't mean you're free to be out of your seats."

A bunch of kids hurry to find their desks and slide into their chairs.

"Please get a pencil out, because today we are having a quiz," says Mr. Gibson.

Uh oh. I had a really busy weekend, and between the mall and soccer and meeting up with Jacob, I didn't exactly end up doing the Science homework. Mr. Gibson doesn't usually check, so I was going to catch up on it tonight. He hadn't said anything about a quiz.

I scramble to get out my pencil and wave my hand into the air. "But you didn't tell us about a quiz, right? So you mean this is a pop quiz?"

"Exactly," says Mr. Gibson.

"Is something wrong?" whispers Torielle.

"Uh, kinda," I say.

"Is it the pop quiz?" asks Torielle.

"Yes," I say. "If he just told us in advance, I'd be feeling a lot more prepared."

"But isn't that the point of a pop quiz?" she says under her breath. Mr. Gibson starts to pass out the quiz.

"The point of not telling us is to surprise us. I don't like surprises," I say with more intensity that I intended. "Personally, I'm against scaring people. But you studied, Torielle. You always study."

Torielle bites her lip. "I did," she says. "I'm way overprepared."

If only that were my problem. This isn't going to be good.

Chapter Seventeen:

The Parent Portal Problem

"Who do you like, Maddie?" asks Katie. It's during lunch the next day. We're sitting at our usual table, only the boys haven't gotten here yet. Who do I like? Well, a boy whose name starts with a J. A boy who texted me last night about why koalas are his favorite animals—because they sleep eighteen to twenty-two hours a day.

I shrug. "I don't know."

"What do you mean, you don't know?" says Torielle. "We've been back to school for a week. You must like someone."

"Maybe Maddie doesn't like anyone," says Jana, coming to my defense.

"Oh, c'mon. Even when you say you don't like someone, you've got some cutie on your radar." Torielle bites into her taco. "Everyone does. Let's be real."

Yes, let's, I think. There *is* someone on my radar.

I see Jacob across the room, heading our way.

"Dish," begs Torielle.

"Later," I say. I nod significantly as Jacob and Lukas head closer.

"Eww, maybe she likes one of Jacob's friends," says Katie.

"Shh," I say, turning red just at the very mention of the name Jacob.

"What do you think of Lukas?" asks Jana.

"Be quiet," I say.

"We're close, aren't we?" says Torielle, raising her eyebrows. "Admit it."

"No! Shh," I beg as Jacob sits down across from me. "The boys are here."

"We *are* here," says Jacob. "Last time I looked." He spins around, scanning behind him and then down the table and Jana giggles. Then he taps himself. "Yup. Definitely here."

Then he peers at me. "So what can't you tell the boys?" He waggles his eyebrows.

"It's girl talk," says Jana, protectively putting her arm around me. "We'll never tell."

"Does it have anything to do with anyone sitting at this table?" asks Lukas.

"Well, in a general way," says Torielle.

I shoot her a *shut up* look, and cough.

"A general boy way," continues Jana. "That's all."

I can feel my cheeks reddening.

"Okay, just checking. Do you want us to leave?" Jacob begins to pick up his tray.

Jana blocks him. "No, don't do that. Then we'd have to hear what Maddie has to say." I know she's just joking, but it still hurts. Especially because what I really want to say, I can't.

In Social Studies, our worksheets are due to Ms. Yoon. Jacob and I turn in our opening statement and rebuttal sheets. Then my stomach drops as I watch him turn in his five sources. I realize I don't have mine—I can see the sheet sitting on my desk at home, but I was so distracted by everything this morning I forgot it.

I wince. "What's wrong?" asks Jacob.

"I left mine at home."

"Oh, shoot."

Ms. Yoon goes down the aisle collecting the homework.

I raise my hand, panicked. "I forgot my sources at home. Can I bring them tomorrow?"

Ms Yoon shakes her head. "I'm sorry, but I can't accept late work. I'm going to have to give you a zero."

"What? A zero!" I've never gotten a zero before.

"Yes, unless you were sick or have a family emergency. It's my policy."

"Can you just mark me down late and take off a few points?" I clasp my hands together.

"I'm sorry."

Jana, who's sitting with Fiona about fifteen feet away near the bookshelf with all of the dictionaries, gives me a sympathetic look. However, Fiona looks oddly pleased, like she thinks I deserve this. How could Jacob be so nice and his cousin so mean? I don't get it.

"Please," I beg. "It won't happen again." I hate sounding so pathetic in front of Jacob and in earshot of half the class.

"There are opportunities to make back some points," says Ms. Yoon. "As I do give extra credit. But for now, I can't give you any credit in the grade book."

Oh no.

Future extra credit will help my overall grade, but it's not what I need right now. Maybe my parents won't see my zero before I can pull my grade up.

I cross my fingers on that hopeful thought.

Unfortunately, hope doesn't get me very far. At home, things aren't going well.

I try to slip away from dinner, but Dad sucks in his breath and glares at me as I begin to walk upstairs to my room. "And who said you were excused from the table, Maddie? Come back and sit down right now. You're not done eating."

He's upset.

Mom's upset.

Elvie's disappointed.

And I'm completely freaked.

My mom happened to go on the parent portal this afternoon. She was admiring all of Elvie's wonderful grades. And then Elvie (thank you very much) showed Mom how to get on the Northborough Middle School portal.

That's when she saw my two terrible, horrible, no good, very bad grades.

My failing grade on my pop quiz, and my zero for resources in Social Studies.

When Dad came home from his law firm, Mom conferred with him right before dinner. They were not happy. They decided I needed consequences. Big ones.

Until I pull up my grades (everything must be a B or above), I'm grounded. That means no going to Jana's party. That means no sleepover. That means no seeing friends. No phone, either. The only thing I can do is schoolwork.

In front of me is *ropa vieja*—shredded brisket in tomato sauce, topped with slices of green olives, all over rice and peas. It's my great-grandma's recipe from Cuba, Mom's *abuelita*. Usually I love it. But tonight I can't eat a bite.

"I said to sit down," says Dad.

"Fine," I say. It's not fair. Elvie might always get good grades, but she's not perfect or anything. Sometimes when my parents think she's studying, she's really playing a game on the computer or group texting with her friends. Plus, recently, she's always late getting home. And sure, Mom has gotten huffy, but they haven't grounded her.

I want to go up to my room so I can get some air. Down here, I feel like I'm underwater, holding my breath.

"Maddie, we were having a discussion," says Dad. "We were in the middle of something."

Elvie takes a bite of peas and rice. "Maddie, if you don't do well in middle school, you'll get further and further behind. You'll never get into the right track at high school."

"Mom, tell her to stop," I plead.

"Elvie, we didn't ask for your opinion," says Mom.

"I'm just offering my wisdom," says Elvie.

"More like bossiness," I say, then I explode. "How come you don't ever notice when she does something wrong? She didn't put away the dishes because she was late getting back from school. But you always notice if I do the smallest thing. You go crazy!"

"Well, now you're going to your room," roars Dad.

The next morning, Mom's standing on the other side of the bathroom door. "Honey, we need to talk."

"I'm in the shower," I say. The water roars out of the spigot, muffling my mother's response. I'm pretty sure she's telling me to turn off the water.

"You want me to go to school with dirty hair?" My stomach tightens as I hear stomping feet coming toward the bathroom door.

"Two minutes, and then that water turns off," growls Dad.

I desperately want to text Jana and let her know how crazy my parents are being. Tears well up in my eyes.

In the shower, I think about everyone having a great time at Jana's party without me. Creating new inside jokes that I'll have no idea about. They'll take tons of pictures, and everyone will see them, and I won't be in any. My breath starts getting jerky, like I've been running for miles and miles.

On the other side of the bathroom door, Mom says, "Maddie, I want to once again explain why your father and I grounded you. It's beca—"

"It's because you hate me," I shout. "You don't want me to have any friends!" Water dribbles down my back.

I turn off the water, wrap myself in a towel, and fling open the bathroom door.

Mom stands there in the hallway, biting her bottom lip and shaking her head. Dad stands next to her. "We don't hate you," she says.

"Oh yeah? Then why are you ruining my life?" My voice comes out in gasps. My head is freezing.

"You have done this to yourself, Maddie," huffs Dad. He's huffing so much little bits of shaving cream flutter off his jaw like clumps of snow.

As if things weren't already stressful enough with Jana, now I have to miss her party. Why are my parents doing this to me?

Chapter Eighteen: Unfairness

"Are your parents really mad?" asks Jana the next morning.

I twirl my locker combination furiously. "They're not happy." I pull some books out of my backpack. "My parents said that until I bring my grades up, I'm grounded."

"What?" Jana stomps her foot, indignant. "That's crazy. In every class? What does that mean? Can you still come to my party?"

"Well, I can if I can get my grades up by this Friday." I shrug. "Ha ha. So like instantly all to A's and B's in three days."

"That's so unfair," says Jana. "I mean, some teachers don't even post quizzes right away and others take forever to grade. You might be doing really well, but the parent portal won't even reflect it."

Katie and Torielle meet us by the lockers and Jana fills them in on the horrible news. They both hug me and tell me they're sorry.

"It's just those two classes, right?" asks Katie.

I nod. "You can do this," says Torielle.

"But probably not by this weekend," I say, swallowing hard.

"I should speak to my mom about this," says Katie. "Teachers should be required to post their grades immediately. Otherwise, it's just unfair. How can you know?"

"Well, that's all well and fine. But right now . . ." I shake my head and start to sniffle. "It's probably too late for me."

Jana's eyes grow wide. "What if I move my slumber party to later this month?"

"Don't do that, Jana." Leaning back against my locker, I shake my head. "Your parents already rented the karaoke machine from that company. Really. Don't. Maybe, somehow, I can pull my grades up."

"Gosh, I hope so," says Katie.

"So harsh," says Torielle.

"I know," I say. "And I would have texted but they took away my phone last night."

"No phone too?" Jana looks indignant. "This is crazy town."

"Luckily, it was just for last night. I talked to my mom this morning and convinced her that not having a phone would be dumb. Since what if they want to get in touch with me?"

"Well, that's good," says Jana. "But I still can't believe they grounded you. I'm so sorry. I wish I had reminded you to bring in that list of resources to Ms. Yoon."

My shoulders slump. "No, I should have remembered on my own."

A couple of eighth-grade girls in their lacrosse hoodies stream past us as Torielle rummages through her locker to fish out her books. "You should ask your teachers if you can do extra credit."

"That's a good idea," I say. "I'll do that. I only need to worry about Social Studies and Science. I'm doing okay in all the rest of my classes." I slip my backpack on my shoulder. "My parents don't want me to go to soccer or even my ceramics class. They say I need to focus *only* on my academics."

"Wow," says Torielle over the increasing noise in

the hallway as more kids pour into school. "That's craziness." She slams her locker shut.

"You can do it, Maddie." Jana hugs me, which makes me feel better. Then she un-Velcros her lunch bag and pulls out a brownie. "For you," she says. "A happy." A *happy* is something we give each other when we are feeling down.

I can feel a smile crawl over my face. "Really?"

"Yeah," she says. "Believe me, I really want to eat it, but I want you to be happy even more."

I might not get to go to Jana's slumber party, but I sure know I have an awesome BFF.

Before Social Studies starts, I ask Ms. Yoon what I can do to make up for my zero. She strolls over to my desk and explains that while I can't completely make it up, I can earn extra credit by creating a chart mapping out the four-step process of delivering a debate. It will also help me prepare for our debate, which is coming up so soon: next Monday. That's just five days! My stomach twists at the very thought.

Jacob pulls out his binder. "Can I do it too?"

"Yes, in fact, everyone can," says Ms. Yoon. She actually announces to the entire class that this extra credit is available to anyone who wants to do it. But it must be turned in by Friday morning.

"That's a lot of work," I say.

"It's actually quite simple," counters Ms. Yoon.

For her, maybe.

But I know I'll do it. Even if I have to stay up all night, I'll do it.

Before Science class starts, I also ask Mr. Gibson if I can do extra credit.

He looks up from reading some biography about some science genius.

"Sure," he says, picking up his coffee cup. "Construct a poster illustrating the phases of mitosis. I'd like the four basic phases: prophase, metaphase, anaphase, and telophase." He pauses to take a sip of coffee. "Also break up prophase to include prometaphase. I'd like it in all sequential order, of course. And everything labeled and in full color." His mustache waggles as he grins. "And that's all."

"Okay," I say and sit back down. I know what I'll be doing all afternoon.

In turns out that writing the four-step debate process takes me two hours. So it's not crazy terrible. But it's not easy, and it makes me think about how everyone will be watching me. It won't be like now, by myself at home. Working on the Science poster takes me three and a half hours. While I'm working, my friends text me and so does Jacob—which gives me mini breaks while I grind away.

I learn some cool facts, like that every organism goes through cell division. While I'm coloring a centrosome yellow in my cell diagram, Dad comes up and makes some dumb jokes, like, "Want to make like an amoeba and split?" Elvie and I both giggle.

That's because we're both working side by side. Actually, I understand her a little bit more now. My sister works really hard. For me, this is an insanely long time to be doing homework, but for her this is normal. It's exhausting. And while I don't think it's fair that she sometimes gets out of chores because of her AP workload, I do understand how she feels that she doesn't have time.

After I finish, I'm totally wiped out. I go to bed at ten-thirty, an hour after my official bedtime.

Handing in the extra credit at Social Studies on Thursday goes well. Lots of other kids did it too, including Jacob and Fiona. Jana didn't, though, since she already had an A. I guess Fiona wanted an A-double-plus.

I shuffle up to Ms. Yoon's desk and ask her if she would add the extra credit to her online grade book right away. She tells me that she's got a very busy afternoon since she's preparing for a teacher conference, but she'll make a good effort to do it by early next week.

"That will be too late. Can you do it sooner? Please?" My voice rises in panic.

"How much sooner?"

"Like this afternoon?"

"I'll try," she says. "But no promises, Maddie."

"Thank you," I say, and I give her my friendliest, most dedicated-student smile ever. It's funny, I've never been the type of person who kisses up to teachers by being all cute and enthusiastic. That's usually Jana's department. But with my crush and my new eager attitude, I'm feeling more and more like my best friend each day. It's kind of weird.

The last period at school, I present Mr. Gibson with my poster. He's writing some science-y terms on the whiteboard with a green dry-erase marker.

"Here," I say, leaning my poster against my knee. I did it on foam core board so it would be extra sturdy.

His mouth drops open in surprise. "I didn't think you'd do it. Wow, Maddie." He leans down to examine the different phases of cell division on my poster. "I especially like that you used different colored pencils to delineate the different parts. We'll be getting to that in a couple of units. But I have to say, this is above and beyond, especially since I was half-joking about it."

"So it was a joke?" I sputter.

"Well, I wasn't planning on teaching mitosis until after Thanksgiving break, so maybe we can use your poster when we get there."

"So do I still get extra credit?"

"Absolutely," he says.

"Can you add the extra credit right away, so it's available on the parent portal? Please."

He narrows his eyes. "Are you up to something?"

I clasp my hands together. "I just want my parents to see."

He caps the dry-erase marker. "Okay, you got it." He cups his mouth. "But don't let the word out that I'd putting my grades up right away. Heh, heh. You people might get used to it."

I laugh, sort of. According to Katie, teachers should put up grades right away. Sometimes putting up grades is your benefit, though, and sometimes it's definitely not.

Chapter Nineteen: Good News

"Good news," I say on Friday morning. I'm standing in front of Jana's locker. She's neatening her stack of books on her top shelf. "My parents said since I raised my grades, I'm no longer grounded, and I can go to the party!"

"*What?*" Jana's whirls around and hugs me. We're jumping up and down together. "That's incredible!" We stop jumping to catch our breath. "So, the extra credit worked."

"Yes, Torielle's a genius. Somehow I convinced both Mr. Gibson and Ms. Yoon to put my extra credit up on the parent portal right away. My parents said as long as I do well in school today and don't do anything stupid—like refuse to do my chores—I'm going to your party!" I dance in place. I'm that happy.

Jana dances with me. Then she pauses and wags a finger at me. "Okay, just whatever you do, don't mess up between now and tomorrow night. You're not allowed to do anything wrong."

I laugh. "I promise," I say. "I'll be a model student. A perfect human being. *Nothing* is going to mess this up!"

I'm so excited that I don't even care that much that it's almost debate day. I know this weekend will go by super fast because of Jana's party. And then before I know it, it'll be Monday—debate time. But I don't worry about it right now because good news flows through me and around me and surrounds me in a protective bubble of happiness.

When I arrive at my advisory, a small bakery box sits on my desk. It's white, and there's a sticker on it that says *The Friendly Bean*. There's also a sticky note that says *Maddie*.

I turn to the kids who sit around me. "Did you see who put this here?"

Nobody has any clue.

I sit and just stare at the box. Why? What? Who?

With my fingernail I cut the Scotch tape and open up the box. A pumpkin spice muffin is nestled inside.

It has to be from Jacob! Last night we had been texting. I had been telling him how nervous I was getting about the debate. And he was trying to get me to relax. He admitted that last year he had gotten nervous too, and the big trick was just to imagine the audience in their underwear. Then he sent me this really funny song parody on YouTube.

And while we were texting, I got the news about being ungrounded and told him. This muffin is probably to celebrate that.

I squeal and then immediately clap my hand over my mouth. Everyone turns to stare at me.

"Is it your birthday?" someone asks.

I shake my head no. It's just probably the best day of my life. I can't believe it. Jacob bought me a muffin, my very favorite—the one I had when we first met. And he somehow snuck into my advisory unseen and placed it here for me to find.

But why?

Because he likes you, says a little voice in my head.

It could be to just pump you up, counters another voice. *He knew how upset you had been about being grounded and worried about the debate.*

Either way, it means he's thinking about me. Either he's the best debate partner in the entire world, or he likes me, or both.

My stomach flutters, like some invisible force is stirring up my insides.

I close the bakery box and carry it with me to my next class.

Pretty much through the rest of the morning, I just stare at the muffin. I can't eat it because it's so perfect looking—puffed-out deliciousness topped with swirly cream cheese icing and orange sprinkles. At least three guys ask me for a bite of whatever is in the box.

Ha! There's just no way.

Carrying the box toward the caf, I realize I should pack it away. I definitely don't want Jana to see it.

But on the other hand, I want to ask Jacob about it so, so, so badly.

Reluctantly, I put the box inside my backpack and join everyone at the lunch table over by the Fixings Bar.

"Feeling better about the debate?" asks Jacob.

I give him a thumbs-up and an extra wide smile, so he'll know just how happy I am.

"You don't seem nervous," says Jana, taking a bite of her salad.

I shake my head. "Well, I wouldn't say that. Let's just say I'm feeling very positive today. I'm so happy to be un-grounded."

"I'm glad," says Jana.

Katie and Torielle discuss this TV show on Netflix that they're watching, and Jana and Lukas build a wall between them made entirely of balled-up napkins and salt shakers because, apparently, Jana thinks that Lukas' sloppy joe looks like barf. "I'm seriously going to be sick," Jana says.

"Well, you can't see the sloppy joe anymore," says Lukas.

Jana plugs her nose and waves her hand in front of her face. "But I can still smell it." She suddenly pops out of her chair. "I need a good smell." She's giggling now.

"What are you talking about?" says Lukas, shaking his head.

"When Maddie and I went to the mall, I put a couple of perfume samplers in her backpack." Jana unzips my front pocket and pokes around. "I could swear I put them in here."

Before I can move, she unzips the main compartment. "What's this?" Her eyes widen in surprise. "A bakery box?" She grabs the box and plops it on the table. "Hiding something?" she asks.

Jacob looks at me and I look at him. I can feel my face flush.

"Um, no. It just appeared," I manage.

"Magically appeared in your backpack?" says Torielle, turning to study me.

"No, in advisory." I shrug. "I have no idea who it's from."

Katie strokes her chin thoughtfully. "None? Really?"

"Well, maybe—I don't know," I say.

A smile appears on Jacob's face. He leans across the table waving his fork. "I have an idea who—"

"Ow!" I yell, holding my stomach. "It really hurts." I jump up, groaning.

"What?" says Jana.

"My stomach," I moan. "It's all cramped up." And that part's not exactly a lie. It's more like an exaggeration. I clap my hand on my forehead. "Maybe I'm a little hot too." I grab my lunch sack and sling my backpack over my shoulder. "I think I should go visit the nurse," I say.

"It's probably just nerves because of your debate coming up," says Katie. "Just a few more days."

"Maybe," I say, relieved that nobody is discussing the pumpkin spice muffin any more.

Jana jumps up. "I'm going with you to see the nurse. You shouldn't be alone."

"Thanks," I say.

Jacob's forehead wrinkles in concern. "Your face is all red. Do you need some ice?"

Yes, my face is red, but not because of a stomach virus or a fever. Red because of embarrassment.

"Don't worry, I'm sure I'll be fine," I say.

In the nurse's office, I hop up on the patient table. The paper crinkles underneath me as I shift around to get comfortable.

Jana sits upright on the edge of a nearby chair. "We've been waiting forever."

"Um, no. More like three minutes."

We both laugh. Jana is not known for her patience.

"Are you any better?" Jana asks.

"A little, actually." I push my hair behind my ears.

"You're a lot less red." *Because Jacob isn't around,* I think.

We share earbuds and listen to this new song from our favorite group, and we're swinging our legs and snapping our fingers when Mrs. Krauss, the school nurse, sweeps into the room. She's wearing a stretchy pair of blue pants and a t-shirt with ladybugs. Her eyeliner is so thick it looks like war paint. Her hair is dyed so white-blond it glows. But the scary thing is you can see her roots, which are chocolate brown.

"Girls, put that phone away," Mrs. Krauss says as she grabs a clipboard and adjusts the stethoscope around her neck. "Just because this is the nurse's office doesn't mean it's not school. The next time I see your phone out I'm going to put it in my box." She points to a box covered in smiley-face wrapping paper. "I'd hate to do that." She takes my temperature even though it's my stomach that hurts, which I told her right when I came in.

Mrs. Krauss glances at both of us. "Are you both sick?"

"No, just me," I say.

Jana stares at up at Mrs. Krauss and says in concern, "Maddie's stomach is really hurting. A really bad cramp."

"Well, aren't you a good friend? If there's a serious problem with Maddie here, she'll need to go see her doctor." She studies me. "How about I call your parents to get them to pick you up? You don't have a temperature, but you'll want to find out what is causing the cramps." She pauses. "Is there anything going on at school or home? Unexpected stress?"

"We have a debate in Social Studies on Monday," says Jana. "And Maddie's afraid of public speaking."

I can speak for myself, I want to say, but I don't.

The expression on the nurse's face changes. She pats my shoulder. "It could be a case of nerves, honey. You might try some deep breathing. And some creative visualizations. My daughter, who's in graduate school, has been taking some mindfulness training and it's really helping her." She studies me again. "Still want me to call your parents?"

I shrug. "Um, you know, it's weird, but since I came in here, I'm suddenly feeling much better. It's like my stomach is pretty much all better."

"Oh really! I'm so glad to hear that. Just keep on breathing, okay, pumpkin?"

I flush. Did she really just call me pumpkin?

When Jana and I stroll back into the hallway, we both admit that Mrs. Kraus is nicer than her reputation. Even if she's a little odd.

"Please don't let me think that bright peach lipsticks looks good when I get to be her age," says Jana.

"I know, and those thick lines under her eyes." I shake my head.

Pivoting around the corner, we start skipping. Jana loops her arm into mine and we're laughing. I've got my earbuds in and I'm listening to a different song by the Ramon Project. After hearing "Lemon Ginger Afternoon" about a hundred times, I've started listening to some of their earlier songs. Suddenly, Jana is poking me. I take out my earbuds.

A familiar voice behind us says, "It's a miracle! You're now one hundred percent better."

I whip around and almost have a heart attack. It's Jacob.

He grabs my earbuds and puts the left one close to his ear. "Wow. You're listening to some early Ramon Project. I knew you'd love them after I sent you 'Lemon Ginger Afternoon.' You're hooked!" He grins, looking proud of himself.

But Jana isn't grinning. She's frowning. I had told Jana that I had just stumbled upon that song. Now she knows I lied.

"I came down to check on you," says Jacob, smiling at me. He's oblivious to Jana's glares in my direction. "But I know you're okay now."

Jacob was coming down to check on me? Normally, I'd be thrilled, but right now I just feel like fainting. Suddenly I want to go straight back to the nurse's office.

"Y-yeah, it's a miracle," I say, studying my hands.

"I hope it wasn't the muffin I gave you that made you sick," says Jacob.

"Er, no," I squeak. I can feel my face turning red.

Jana's face is red too. Mouth puckering, she glares at Jacob. "*You* gave that muffin to Maddie?"

"Um, yeah." He shrugs, clearly baffled why Jana is so bewildered. "Pumpkin spice is her favorite, so, yeah. It was a combo 'happy un-grounding' and 'thank you.'"

"For what?" asks Jana.

Jacob looks at me. "Well, Maddie wasn't exactly subtle about decorating my locker. So that."

"You think that *Maddie* decorated your—" Jana shudders.

Jacob turns to me, his brows lifted in confusion. "You did it, right?"

"Well, I did," I admit. "But it was with Jana—" I pause midsentence. Jana has fled. She's full-out running, like she's a defender chasing after a breakaway forward during a high-stakes soccer game.

"Gotta go. I'll explain later." I race down the hall. My backpack thumps painfully against my spine, but I don't care.

I catch up with Jana by the Student Council bulletin board. "Look," I say, bending over, panting and out of breath. "I can explain everything."

Jana backs away from me. "I don't care what you have to say! You are a terrible friend! You lied! A lot! You've betrayed me! You're officially uninvited to my slumber party! And P.S.—I'm inviting Fiona instead." Then she walks away from me and disappears around the corner.

Chapter Twenty:
Steamed Up

At home after school, I storm into the bathroom and slam the door. Then I jump into the shower, turn the water as hard as it will go, and shout out my frustration to the universe. Screaming in the shower is a great strategy, because nobody can really hear you. Steam wisps into the bathroom, and the jet of water pounds my head.

I'm not going to the slumber party.

I'm probably not going to be Jana's best friend anymore, either.

Is Jana now going to tell Fiona all her secrets instead? Was I going to be replaced, just like that? It was so ironic. I hadn't told Jana my secret because

I was trying to follow the BFF Code and be a good friend, and I didn't want to be like Fiona the Betrayer. I kept my mouth shut for her. And look what that got me! Whereas look what being a betrayer got Fiona—apparently, new BFF status!

And what about Katie and Torielle? Were they going to stop being friends with me too?

Even though there's steam everywhere, my throat feels completely dry.

"Maddie, can you please wrap up your shower?" says Mom through the door. "You've been in there forever."

"I'm almost done."

"Now," says Mom.

Can't I have even a few moments of hot water and steam and tears to myself? No. Apparently not.

I feel like I'm alone on a mountaintop and screaming my head off, but nobody can hear me. And Jana, Fiona, Torielle, and Katie are on another mountaintop, dancing around with lots of Cool Ranch Doritos, having a high-altitude party—one that I'm not invited to.

Tonight, the night of Jana's slumber party, will be long and boring and dark and awful. It seems pretty obvious now that Jacob likes me, but I just feel way too embarrassed to talk to him about any of this. Plus, it doesn't make up for losing my friends.

I don't know what to do. I flip through Mom's self-help books, and then Google some advice boards. I use a fake name and post my problems online to see what people suggest.

None of the advice is very helpful.

Don't think of yourself. You'll eventually get over it.

Start over and make new friends.

Instead start being extra helpful around the house. Really? How will that help?

Don't wait to be asked, just do things.

I'm doing something, all right. I'm sitting on my bed doing nothing, while all of my friends are having fun.

Late Sunday morning, I reach for the iced tea on my nightstand. I try to take a sip, but I can barely swallow.

I've had my phone with me all morning, waiting for someone to check in. The truth is that Jacob did text me on Friday and Saturday. We didn't talk about what happened, though. We just chatted about soccer. Best family vacations. His was Costa Rica. Mine was going to Quebec City during Winter Carnival. It cheered me up to text with him.

But I really miss my friends, especially Jana.

I thought that at least Torielle might be in touch. Or maybe Katie. I hope for that ping, but nothing. Silence. My heart sinks.

Jana's Snappypic feed is filled with photos of the party.

I know they couldn't help posting photos of how much fun they were having at the party. But it's even worse because I helped plan it. I helped shop for it. I made and designed the spinner for the nail polish game—which, in the photos, looks like it was so much fun.

I slump into the family room and flop down onto the sofa. I don't pick up a magazine, turn on the TV, or even slide my phone out of my pocket. I can't bear to look at any more photos of my besties having an awesome time without me.

I kick off my shoes, and they clunk down onto the floor.

Morty noses over and put his chin onto my lap. His brown eyes implore me to pet him. I scratch his head and then push him away.

"Sorry, Morty," I say, immediately feeling like the worst pet owner in the world. "I just can't right now."

Morty stares at me, his pink tongue lolling.

To make things worse, I think about the debate. Tomorrow. As in the very next day. How can I possibly debate now? How can I have logical thoughts or present an organized argument when I'm such a mess?

And to make matters worse, I have to go head-to-head with Jana.

Can tomorrow get any worse?

I flip over and my face smushes into a cushion. It smells dusty, and I cough. I lay there for what could be seconds or minutes, and then someone is lightly shaking me.

"What's wrong, Maddie?" I glance up. Elvie stands over me, a concerned look on her face.

"Nothing."

She plops down at the end of the couch. "Really? C'mon. I know you better. What's up?"

My voice catches but I manage to tell her everything that happened. She listens, petting Morty the whole time.

"Remember that time that Caroline and I had a fight?" she says.

"I think so."

"Oh, c'mon. It was last year, and we were going to throw a surprise birthday party for her boyfriend, Tariq, only she did it without me?"

"Yeah, I do."

"I wish I didn't." She pauses and winces. "So, I had drawn up all of these plans for the party, and she had seemed so excited. But then Caroline went ahead and picked a random date for it, which wasn't even Tariq's birthday, and literally tells me that morning to show up later. And she didn't do any of the stuff we'd planned for it. I was so mad. We had such a big blow-up about it. But later I realized that it wasn't really about me. I had wanted to have a big party, but Caroline was embarrassed about her house—it's really small. So she wanted to keep the guest list small too."

"Oh," I say. "But Jana doesn't have a small house. Her house is really big, actually. A two-story. Way bigger than our ranch."

"Maddie, that's not what I mean exactly, except there might be other stuff going on with people. Sometimes you just have to forgive, that's all."

"Okay, yeah. I get it." I pick up the remote to turn

on the TV. It's Sunday and I'm allowed to watch two hours of Netflix, after all.

"And one more thing," adds Elvie.

"What?" I ask.

My sister raises her hand and dashes out of the room. "Hold that thought."

I hear her clomping up the stairs, and two minutes later she's back with a teal blue fabric headband. "This headband would look so good with that sweater." She gestures at the sweater I'm wearing. It's also teal.

"You're right," I say.

She smiles. "I know."

"Maybe I'll wear it tomorrow. For my debate."

She gives me a thumbs-up and heads back to her room, for more studying, of course.

The headband is a perfect color blue, I think. Just like the color of Jacob's eyes.

Thinking about Jacob just reminds me of Jana, though, which reminds me of my mess. I know my sister was trying to help, but I don't think anything can help right now.

"There's one more thing I wanted to tell you." Elvie is suddenly back. She looks nervous. She sits down on the couch. "There's a reason why I've been getting home late recently."

"It's because of your study groups, right?"

Elvie fiddles with the threads on a throw cushion. "Actually, no. I've been working two days a week at the Friendly Bean."

"What? Really?"

"Remember that *Help Wanted* sign?"

I nod. "I think so."

"Well, I applied the day after I took you there, that weekend before school started. I've been working there after school. I wanted to start earning my own money, but Mom and Dad didn't believe that I could keep my grades up and do all the stuff that I do if I also got a job. But I knew differently. I had to prove it to them."

I stare at my sister. "Wow. You've been keeping that secret this whole time!"

"Yup," she says. "And I really like working there. They've taught me how to make the perfect cup of coffee. There's a real art to it. I'm not too good with the steaming machine yet, but I'm getting there. I've been saving a lot of money too. At the rate I'm going, I'll be able to buy an electric bass for sure."

"That's awesome, Elvie. Can you get free stuff there?"

She shakes her head. "But I do get an awesome employee discount. And sometimes they have day-old desserts they give us for a treat."

"Are you going tell Mom and Dad?"

"Yes," she says. "As soon as I can work up my nerve. It's been driving me crazy, keeping this inside. Really, I don't like lying, or avoiding telling the truth. It makes me feel guilty all the time."

"Your grades are still perfect, aren't they?"

She smiles. "Yeah, pretty much. I just got an A on my AP US History test."

"I think Mom and Dad are going to be fine with your little secret."

"I certainly hope so," she says.

"Well, what are you waiting for?"

"You think I should tell them now?" My sister looks worried.

"Yes," I say. "Now. You don't want them finding out another way. Trust me."

Chapter Twenty-one: REBUTTAL TROUBLE

On Monday, I duck into Social Studies and see that the layout of the room has been completely altered. I'm so nervous I couldn't eat lunch. Well, okay, two bites of the sandwich that Mom made for me. Even that is churning in my stomach.

I'm feeling light-headed. I blink and try to steady myself.

Hold it together, I tell myself. The only good thing that has come out of this whole mess is that Elvie actually told our parents about her job. At first they were really upset that she hadn't told them before, and they were especially angry that she had lied to them and said she'd been home late because of study group or club meetings. But Elvie explained how she wanted more independence and how she was old enough to choose some of her activities. And she showed them how her grades hadn't dropped at all.

Once Mom and Dad got over the initial surprise, they were actually pretty impressed. Dad wanted Elvie to make him a cappuccino right at home, but Elvie calmly explained we didn't have the right equipment for that. My parents needed to visit her at the Friendly Bean, and they planned on doing that this weekend.

Elvie was lucky that her secret didn't result in the mess that mine did.

The desks in Social Studies have been pushed out of the way, except for a few in front of the whiteboard. Thirty chairs form a semicircle around the perimeter of the room. In addition to the HISTORY ROCKS banner and the poster featuring Roman soldiers in their armor, there is also a giant banner that reads DEBATE TIME!

Yes, it's today, our big debate. Jacob and I are going up against Jana and Fiona. My stomach tightens. It all feels like some cruel joke.

I look around for Jana. She and Fiona the Betrayer

stand in the back, arranging note cards into neat stacks along the counter.

Jana catches my eye and glares at me.

She hates me. Completely hates me.

I shuffle past a group of kids standing in the center of the classroom and move toward Jacob, who's over by the pencil sharpener. All around me, students chatter, clearly curious to watch the first debates of the year. We don't yet know the order of who's going today. Just that we're going. That's enough for me. I don't think knowing would help me relax. A few kids hurry past me to speak to Ms. Yoon, who is at her desk, folding placards that say "pro/proposition" and "con/opposition."

Jacob paces, probably practicing his opening argument. Taking a shuddering breath, I walk up to him.

Out of the corner of my eye, I see Jana heading our way.

"Hey, Maddie," Jacob says, running his fingers through his hair.

"Hey." I shrug off my backpack and drop it by my feet. I keep my eyes on Jana.

"What happened to everyone during lunch today?" asks Jacob.

"Oh, right. I forgot to say I was in the library," I tell him, lowering my voice. "I wanted to prepare. I don't know where everyone else went." Probably the girls' bathroom, I think, to complain about me. Even though Jacob and I have been texting, we've managed to avoid talking about my fight with Jana. Probably because at some level he knows he's the reason for it.

Jana steps up to the pencil sharpener.

"Ready for the big showdown?" asks Jacob.

"Sure." Now it's my turn to pace. My throat feels tight, like I'm coming down with a cold. Even though I know I'm not. I can feel Jana's eyes like lasers burning the back of my head.

"Oh, look," says Jacob, turning to face Jana as the sharpener whirs. I turn too. "It's the enemy, the pro side." He smiles at Jana.

"That's right," answers Jana, her voice hard. "We're the pros and you guys are just cons." She blows—actually more like huffs—on her now extra-pointy pencil and marches back to Fiona.

My face heats up as we walk toward our seats.

"Wow, Jana seems ready to attack," says Jacob. "She's taking this very seriously."

"Uh huh." I sink into my chair. "She sure is."

Jacob pulls a binder out of his backpack. "Maddie, are you all right? You look a little"—he pauses—"pale. Are you feeling sick again or something?"

"I'm fine," I say, because Jacob is the very *last* person I can tell what's really wrong. I wish I actually had been sick on Friday. If the nurse had sent me home, then I would have never run into Jacob, and Jana would have never run into the truth.

Speaking of Jana, she's high-fiving Fiona about something. Something about me, no doubt.

Unzipping my backpack, I pull out my note cards and shakily stack them on my lap. "Do you think Ms. Yoon will be able to tell if we read from our notes?" I whisper, quickly glancing back at our teacher.

"Definitely," says Jacob.

The bell rings to start class, and Ms. Yoon stands in front of her desk. She places the pro and con placards onto the four empty desks. She holds up a small, egg-shaped timer. "We're going to start right away, since we need to get through three debates today. The first group will be debating whether we should have school uniforms." Ms. Yoon pauses and then pats the four empty desks in front of the whiteboard. "So, Landon, Bryce, Risa, and Keisha, come on up. You're all in the hot seats."

There's cheering and a few sighs as the first group proceeds to the front of the class. I glance over at Jana and see she's frowning. She probably just wants to go first and just get it over with.

The dueling teams sit down and place their notes on their desks.

"After this group," continues Ms. Yoon, "We'll have the teams arguing for and against year-round school. Then we'll have the group debating school security cameras."

I look directly at Jacob and he looks at me. Wow. Okay, momentarily, I had somehow forgotten how bright his eyes were. It's crazy, but his lashes are way darker than mine. And mine are pretty dark.

"We're last," he whispers. "More time to prepare."

"More like more time to get nervous," I say under my breath as Ms. Yoon goes over how the debate will proceed.

"Please, no talking," Ms. Yoon says, putting her finger to her lips. "I know you've heard the rules before. The format of this debate has been altered from what you might see with our after-school debate society, but the basic principles are the same. The opening statement is five minutes. This will include a hook, the body of your argument with three main points backed by evidence, then a closing summary of your position. The rebuttal, which will be four minutes, follows, and is, as we discussed, impromptu. However, you should have anticipated your opponent's arguments already. You can also take notes while your opponent presents his or her opening statement and the body of the argument. The rebuttal team members will also present a closing statement. This should be something emotional that persuades the audience that you have won the debate."

She waves her timer. "I'll let you know when you're almost out of time by holding up my fingers. Also, another thing. Audience members can't speak, but they may stamp their feet if they like a point. Traditionally in debate, we pound on our desks, but we're modifying it a bit. In addition, everyone in the audience must write down one question they'd like to ask the proposition and one question for opposition. At the end of the class, please hand them to me.

These will be graded." She peers around the room. "Any questions before we begin?"

There are a bunch of questions, including dumb ones like, *If I'm debating do I have to write down an audience question?* After she finishes responding to all the questions, it's finally time.

The debates officially begin.

Fiona keeps on looking back at me and then at Jacob. Her eyes practically bounce like ping-pong balls from him to me. Jana obviously told her everything that happened.

I feel queasy. Jana has been confiding in Fiona the Betrayer, who is also Jacob's cousin. Does Jacob now know everything too? A surge of anger shoots through me, and I can barely concentrate on the debate going on in front of the class. I'm supposed to be listening as an active audience member. But I just can't.

Jacob studies me a moment and scrawls in his notebook. *What's Going On?*

Nerves, I scribble back, and make a happy face even though I'm not feeling so happy. Okay, I guess he doesn't know.

He glances up to make sure Ms. Yoon is not looking, and then writes, *You'll be Awesome*.

I give a wavery smile and try to listen to the debate. Risa speaks emphatically and slowly. I hear phrases like "Why spend money?" and "Fashion is expensive," but I'm not exactly following her.

I try to focus for just long enough to write down my two required questions to turn in to Ms. Yoon. When I'm done with that, the rest of debate just sounds like "blah blah blah" punctuated by the occasional polite stomping of feet by the audience and banging on desks by the debate team. I can't concentrate. I can only feel Jana's burning stare.

Plus, I'm sitting right next to Jacob.

This is only the second time I've sat next to him.

Normally during Social Studies our desks have been pushed together so that we face each other, like at a dinner table. In the caf, Jana always made sure to sit next to him.

I'm so hyperaware of Jacob's nearness. His leg is only inches from my leg. Even his breathing is distracting.

He starts to tap my clog with the front of his running shoe.

I stiffen. Any other time, I'd be thrilled, but I can feel Jana's eyes on me. She whispers to Fiona, who seems to have been fully restored to the number-one best-friend position.

Ms. Yoon announces that the year-round school debate group is now up.

That means in about ten minutes it will be our turn. I try to take deep, calming breaths. It doesn't help.

There's lot of fidgeting in the classroom. Paper rustles. Chairs scrape on the floor. The thumping of feet on the floor during exciting points gets a little louder. It's not because the arguments aren't that interesting, it's just that everyone's getting a little bored. By the time it's our turn to go up, everyone will be dying for class to be over.

I once again focus on the debate long enough to write out two questions. Max Fisker is saying something about how having school during the summer would be awesome since "nobody would forget everything they learned during long vacations."

While he's finishing up his argument, Fiona brushes her hair. Jana applies lip gloss.

I press my fingers to my own lips. They're paper dry. I could use some lip gloss myself. But there's no way I'm putting on makeup in front of Jacob.

A few minutes later, Jana and Fiona are writing furious notes to each other. They pass them back and forth whenever Ms. Yoon turns her head. I'm sure they are writing all about me.

"Just three more minutes," whispers Jacob. "They're going down." He nods at Jana and Fiona.

I give him a thumbs-up.

My ears burn. My throat constricts.

All I know is I didn't intentionally betray anyone. The opposite, actually. Even though I had a crush on Jacob first, I went along with Jana and the BFF Code and tried to support her crush. But who really decorated Jacob's locker for his birthday? Why did Jacob really want to sit with us at lunch? Because of me—that's why. Did I say anything about it? Noooooo.

Someone is shaking me, and I startle. "It's our turn," Jacob says gently. "We're up."

"Oh, right," I manage, jumping up and forgetting about the stack of note cards on my lap. They spill to the floor. As I pick them up, Jana and Fiona cover their mouths to contain their laughter.

Ms. Yoon holds up her timer. "Are we ready to start our last debate?"

Not really.

We all sit down in the desks in front of the whiteboard. Jana knows how much I hate public speaking. She and Fiona probably think I'm going to be really bad.

"Ready to fight?" asks Jacob, his blue eyes intense.

"You bet I am." And this time I'm not telling a lie. This time I mean it.

Jacob's opening argument goes really well. During the body of his argument, he gives the example of a middle school that had cameras installed in the boys' and girls' locker rooms. The cameras filmed girls changing and then unauthorized people downloaded those images, he explained. Hundreds of them.

People bang their feet on the floor and shake their heads, disgusted. Score for Jacob. Meanwhile, Jana is busy writing down notes for her rebuttal. Whatever she's writing down pleases her, because she has this smug look on her face.

Jacob ends with, "The real question is what is better—security or freedom? I'm always going to go for freedom." He sits back down and there's more stamping of feet. I pound on my desk.

Fiona is, unfortunately, really good. As she speaks, I'm furiously scribbling down what she says so I can make my counterarguments. It all feels like a game of soccer. Someone attacks and then someone else blocks. The other team takes possession and the pattern begins again.

Before I know it, it's rebuttal time.

It will just be Jana and me for the final showdown.

Jana goes first. She throws back her shoulders and stands up extra straight. "My opponent said that schools without cameras are places of freedom. But you can't be free where there is crime. Knowing that the school has surveillance cameras will allow students, parents, teachers—everybody in a school—a sense of security and safety. They will always know what's *really* going on."

Lots of kids nod. Fiona swells with pride and bangs on her desk in approval. Ms. Yoon writes something down on that spreadsheet of hers.

"My opponent also said that cameras couldn't catch everything," continues Jana. "However, that's not true! There are many tools for capturing criminals and *unwanted* and *disgusting* behavior." Jana's eyes graze a note card on her desk. She talks about fisheye cameras that give 360-degree views and night vision cameras. She explains how cameras send a strong message to criminals that they are unwanted. That video footage will provide proof of wrongdoing.

"With cameras," she says, staring right at me, "you know exactly what's happening. There are no more secrets."

Fiona glares at me. My heart thumps hard.

Jana was not just talking about security cameras, of course.

She was talking about us.

I feel light-headed. Biting my lip, I tell myself to get a grip. I can do this.

Some kids pound on the floor really hard. Others whisper, obviously surprised how heated this is all getting. I'm obviously not.

Jana clasps her hands and smiles knowingly at me. Now it's my turn.

I stand up and slam my stack of note cards onto the chair. Jana thinks there is no way I can do a decent rebuttal. Well, sorry. She is wrong.

"My opponent said that cameras give a sense of security, a sense of safety," I state. "However, that is not true! All cameras do is make everyone paranoid and feel watched. Cameras tell students that they can't be trusted. That kind of atmosphere is bad for education, friendship, and happiness!"

Kids stamp their feet on the floor. Jacob pounds on his desk. Jana's eyes grow big. Fiona's mouth drops open. I can tell they expected me to stammer and squeak like a mouse.

I continue, feeling bolder. "Constantly being watched by a camera makes you feel guilty even before you've done anything wrong. Just because the school has cameras doesn't mean that all is going to be well. FYI, Jana, your example was so off!"

Ms. Yoon holds up her hand. "In debate, please remember not to use names. Thank you."

"Excuse me," I say. "I mean, *my opponent* talked about night vision security cameras, which doesn't make sense. Since when do we go to school at night?" Then I talk about how expensive cameras are. And how it's better to put money toward teachers' salaries. I can see Ms. Yoon smiling at this.

Even more kids stamp their feet on the floor this time. Smiling, Jacob thumps on his desk.

I dig deeper and discuss the expense of maintaining cameras. And how the cameras themselves could be stolen.

I continue, "This is not a war zone. But *my opponent* is turning it into one, and so that's what it'll become. War!"

"Whoa!" someone calls out. Fiona compulsively neatens the stack of note cards she no longer needs. Jana blinks hard. Jacob, on the other hand, looks thrilled.

There's more vigorous banging on the floor. Grinning, Jacob pumps his arm into the air like I've just made an impossible goal.

Ms. Yoon waggles ten fingers at me, which means I have only ten more seconds.

"My opponent said that cameras could be put everywhere," I say. "Sorry, but surveillance cameras are an invasion of privacy. Plus, it's just a set-up for abuse. Imagine how easy it would be for someone to get hold of a certain bit of information and use it against somebody to"—I bang the desk with my fist for emphasis—"completely ruin her life!"

Bryce takes his notebook and uses it like a fan. He nods over at Jana, who is gripping her desk with her hands, and then over at me, my fists still tightly clenched. "Those two need to take it outside," he says. "They're ready to rumble."

"No talking, audience," reminds Ms. Yoon. "Now each of you gets up to one minute to respond. This will be your final point."

Jana starts. "Some people just can't be trusted," she says, crushing the note card in her hand.

Fiona nods her head in agreement.

"If you turn your back for one second," continues Jana, "they do what they're not supposed to do. And they'll never tell you what they're *really* up to. The only way you'll know is if you have a camera to show you, because there's *zero* trust. We need cameras to make sure people follow the rules." When she sits back down in her seat, her face is bright red. The sound of thundering feet fills the room.

"Okay, Maddie, you're up," says Ms. Yoon. "You have one minute for your last statement."

I stand up. "A lack of trust creates a toxic environment," I say. "When there's no trust, people feel like they can't tell anybody anything. So then they do things behind other people's backs. Sometimes there's no other choice! Not having cameras creates a better community."

Lots of kids stomp their feet on the floor and there's even general cheering. Jacob is the loudest, a proud grin on his face. And suddenly a strange thought pops into my mind. I realize that I haven't been nervous. I'm good at debating! And it feels good to be good at it. It's weird to know you're talented at something at the same time you're being upset.

"That was quite a rebuttal, girls," says Ms. Yoon. Others nod in agreement.

Jacob gives me a high five.

But I'm really not feeling so great.

Because Jana is racing out the door. Tears stream down her cheeks.

The bell rings and I can hear Ms. Yoon say, "Girls, is there something else going on?"

But I don't have time to answer. Without a moment's hesitation, I race after Jana.

Chapter Twenty-two: GEESE AND A PUSHY PIGEON

"Jana, we need to talk. This is all just because of a misunderstanding," I say. Somehow, I've cornered her by her locker.

Jana glares at me. "Excuse me," she says icily. What she really means is, *get out of my face.*

I step away from her locker. "Please," I blurt. "I couldn't sleep all weekend."

"Is that supposed to make me feel better?" Jana snarls.

Most of the kids passing by hurry, but a few slow down to stare at the girl drama. I want to crawl inside a locker.

Jana turns her back to me and spins the combination to her locker. "What's there to say?"

So much. Everything.

Jana yanks open her locker door and shoves her backpack onto the hook. "I promised myself I wouldn't talk to you ever again. The only reason I just spoke with you earlier was because I had to, because of the debate. I swore I'd only surround myself with my *real* friends."

I fold my arms. "You mean like Fiona? Yeah, I saw all of those photos on Snappypic. You and Fiona posted like twenty of them. '*Me with my BFF*' and then all of those cheesy red hearts. So much for her being the Betrayer."

Jana breathes slowly. She slams her locker shut with a resounding thud. "It's all messed up." Her eyes look moist, and she rubs them.

Seeing her all emotional gets to me. I start sniffling too. My throat knots.

Kids flood the hall. Eyes are everywhere. I'm feeling like we're in a fishbowl.

"Jana, can we"—I pause and flatten myself against the lockers as a group of sixth-grade boys zoom past with their sharp elbows—"take a walk or sit down somewhere?"

"Fine." She sucks in her cheeks, and my heart lifts just a little.

Together, we move down the hall, navigating around the throngs of other kids, and head outside to the cafeteria patio where there's a bunch of picnic tables. No one else is out there. The wind whips our hair into our mouths and slaps against our skin. The clouds look purple and bruised, like it's about to rain.

Jana plops down onto a picnic table bench.

"I think that's kind of wet," I say, sitting across from her.

She folds her arms. "Whatever. You suddenly care about me now? You're worried? After making it obvious to Jacob that you decorated his locker? And making him think my note was from you!"

"I didn't do that!" I protest.

"Oh, I'm supposed to believe you now? After all the things you've done. All of your flirting with Jacob right in front of my face?"

"Well, you never pay attention. I didn't think you'd even notice."

Jana hops up from the picnic table. "What are you trying to say about me? That I'm a self-centered jerk?

Not a good friend? So, why even be my friend if I'm so horrible?"

"That's not what I'm saying."

She slaps her hands on her hips. "What are you saying?"

I burst into tears. "You're my best friend. I don't want it to be like this. You made a point of putting up those pictures just to hurt my feelings. And guess what? It worked." I pull out a tissue from my backpack and dab at my eyes. "I don't want to be your friend if you treat me like this."

"Well, what do you expect me to do when you steal Jacob?"

"I didn't steal him," I say. "I liked him too, before you even knew him, and he has his own choice about who he likes. But I thought you'd stop liking him. Over the summer you liked Jesse, then you thought Toby was awesome, and then Arnie."

Jana softly laughs. "Well, yeah."

A pigeon lands on the pavement below my feet. "Shoo!" I say, flapping my arm. "There's no food here. Go!" Insistent, the pigeon bobs up and down.

"They're such pests." Jana opens her bag and pulls out the leftover crust from her sandwich. "Here," she says, throwing the crust across the patio. The pigeon is there instantly. "Now he won't bother us for another fifteen seconds."

"How do you know it's a he?"

"Because *he's* a problem bird." She pauses, and I can see that her eyes are moist.

An awkward silence spreads between us. I hear the branches of the trees creaking in the wind.

"I missed you so much during my slumber party," Jana's words gush out in a torrent. "It wasn't the same without you. Every time I was doing my nails and I'd go, 'I really like this flamingo-pink color,' I was also thinking, *so would Maddie*. Or when we were picking out movies to watch—I know how much you like comedies. I was scanning to see the best one, and I realized you weren't there."

"But on Snappypic it looked like you were having *so* much fun." My words sound whinier than I want.

"Trust me"—she shakes her head—"it was just okay. Not great. My dad picked up this pecan cheesecake from Costco, and nobody ate it. The pizza was soggy, and I forgot that Katie was gluten-free. Things just didn't go right. If you had been there, it would've been so much have been better." Her bottom lip quivers. "I miss you sooooo much!"

Then all once Jana starts to cry, noisily, sloppily, with short sucked-in breaths and hiccups.

I hand her a tissue, and we're blowing our noses at the same time.

"We sound like geese," I point out with another hiccup.

"Speak for yourself." I worry she's annoyed, but her lips tug into an almost-smile.

"I miss you. I can't stand us being like this," I say. We're both crying again. It's a good kind of cry, though, like when you come inside a warm room and take off a heavy winter jacket after being in the freezing cold, and you feel so relieved. You're lighter and freer.

The wind picks up. Dry leaves rattle across the patio. It smells crisp and cold and earthy, like fall. Summer has really passed.

The pigeon finally flies away. "We scared him, I guess."

"Good," says Jana.

"So," I say, and hesitate. The silence stretches out between us again.

"So," says Jana.

We have to get to our next classes soon, but I know I have to explain. I have to tell her everything. "I'm really sorry that I kept so many secrets. But it all happened because I didn't want to lose you as a friend," I say. "I was trying not to be a betrayer, like Fiona." Then I go on to describe the whole pumpkin spice scenario at the Friendly Bean. How Elvie gave me big-sister advice to be loyal and follow the BFF Code. How I was trying to tell Jana all about Jacob right away, but she had no service over Labor Day weekend. Then on the first day of school, when we stepped into the caf, just when I was going to tell her about this new adorable guy, she gushes about her new crush—Jacob. Jacob, of all people. There are almost three hundred boys at Northborough Middle and she picked Jacob.

"Oh my gosh." Jana slaps one cheek and then the other. "That's it. I *so* remember. You said you had news." Her eyes narrow in understanding. "You should have just told me. Instead you kept on lying. Even about how you first heard that crazy ginger song." Jana bounces off the bench and starts to jump up and down to keep warm. Neither of us has on warm coats. "Brr, the temperature really dropped."

She rubs her hands together and I'm doing the same. "I'd have been, well, a little upset, if you had told me that day, but I would've understood."

I shake my head. "No, you wouldn't have, Jana. You're used to being the one with all the crushes, and used to guys always liking you. You're so cute and fun and silly. Things usually go your way."

Jana fidgets with the strap on her bag. "Okay, I would've been angry. But I would've come around. Eventually." She thinks for a second. "Now all that stuff about the Friendly Bean makes a lot more sense."

I nod. "Oh, and Elvie works there now!" I go on to describe Elvie's former secret—her job and her plans to learn the electric bass and start her own band. How my parents didn't want her working because they were afraid she couldn't keep up her grades. How she proved them wrong.

"Yay, go Elvie!" says Jana, and she plops back down on the bench.

"I know." I have to keep on pushing my hair out of my face because of the breeze.

"Can we get a discount at the Friendly Bean now?"

"Maybe." And then I decide to say what I'm truly afraid to ask. "So you're not mad any-more?"

Jana gazes down at her hands pressed against the metal table. "No, I'm not really mad. I mean, I was. I didn't get it." She glances up at me, and her eyes are filled with understanding. "I thought you had gone behind my back. But really, it was a misunderstanding. And it's silly to try to 'claim' a person—plus, Jacob is clearly more interested in you." She pauses. Jana rarely pauses in the middle of talking. She's like one of those Energizer Bunnies that doesn't need a new battery. "Now about my crush—"

"I can so totally tell Jacob, you know, to forget about our whatever, thing. It's so not worth—"

"I don't like him," blurts Jana. "I don't like Jacob."

"What?" Now it's my turn to leap off the picnic table and jump up and down in place to keep warm. "I'm sooooo confused."

"I mean, I did like him. Sure. But there's someone else." She blushes. "Lukas."

"But you always complain about him!"

"Yeah, well, I kind of like him. A lot."

"Really?" I stop bouncing. "Oh my gosh. That's why you asked me what I thought about him!" I cover my mouth. "I totally didn't get it."

She nods and gets a silly grin on her face. "Yes, really. He's so funny. I can't stop laughing when I'm around him. I guess I was annoyed because I didn't want to like him. But I do!"

"So you forgive me?" I ask hopefully.

"I'm really sorry for uninviting you from my slumber party." Jana shakes her head. "It wasn't right."

"Well—" I study the pavement where a line of ants scurry across to the caf. "How were you supposed to know what the truth was if I didn't tell you? Plus I actually think it helped my debate."

"I know," says Jana. "You were so heated up. I've never seen you like that. You were really mad."

"Maddie," I joke. "That's my name."

"Well, you were really good. I'm serious."

I'm thinking again about how at the end of the debate, instead of feeling nervous, I felt strangely confident. It seemed like something I was good at. I kind of want to do more of it. My dad is a litigator—maybe he passed on some of his lawyer genes.

"Thanks. I actually really liked doing it," I say.

"Maybe I won't do indoor soccer over the winter, and I'll go out for the debate team instead. I want to try it out. It just might be my thing."

"That's awesome," says Jana. "I mean, I'll miss you on the soccer team. But that's okay. It's not like I can't see you in school, or hang on the weekends."

"Exactly."

Jana's eyes gleam and her dimples bookend her mouth.

"So, now that we're talking again," I say, smiling, "I can give you this." I unzip my backpack and slip out the wrapped present I have for Jana. "I actually brought it to school, hoping that maybe we could, somehow, make up."

I hand it to Jana and she eagerly tears it open, shredding the purple tissue paper. First she sees the silver key chain that reads *Every tall girl needs a short best friend*. She cracks up. "I love it!"

"There's more," I say. "See?"

Jana paws through the tissue paper and finds a small white box. Lifting the lid, she pulls out the soccer ball necklace. "Wow!" Her whole face lights up. She holds up the necklace, staring. She shakes her head in surprise. "I've been wanting this! I seriously have a desperate need for this necklace. But it was so expensive and—" She studies me, her eyebrows lifting. "How did you know?"

"That day at the mall. Remember? When we were buying stuff for your party and to also decorate Jacob's locker? I saw you staring at this necklace as we passed by the jewelry store. It was pretty obvious you wanted it."

"Only because you're my best friend," she says quietly. "And FYI . . . I knew too."

"What do you mean?"

"I knew that you liked Jacob. And he liked you. I could tell during lunch and Social Studies. At first, I just tried to ignore it. But honestly, it was hard to miss."

At this, butterflies flutter like crazy in my stomach. Everything's all tingly and bubbly. "Really?"

"It's okay. I get it." She studies the present and looks up at me. "I love you."

"I love you too." I bite my bottom lip.

Jana's eyes rise to my hairline. "I really like your headband. It matches your shirt."

"Thanks! Elvie gave it to me." I pull it off and twirl it around.

"Really? She never does stuff like that."

"She was being nice to me." I thought about our conversation in the family room on Sunday. Sometimes you have to just forgive people.

"We are so late to class now, but this was worth it," I say. "Oh, and there's one more thing I have to give you." I let out a happy sigh and throw my arms around Jana. "A giant birthday hug!"

She squeezes me back. "You know, I'm going to have to try that pumpkin spice trick with Lukas."

"It's pretty effective," I admit. "Just make sure it's not a hot drink. I think ice is safer and makes quite an impression. You should find out—"

"Lukas' favorite drink first and then spill it on him!" Jana finishes my sentence and we both crack up.

"Great minds—" I start.

"Think alike!" she cries.

Chapter Twenty-three:
THE SECRET IS OUT

Tuesday speeds by. I feel so much better—relieved, and so happy. I appreciate Jana in a whole new way. How she bounces when she walks, how she texts to remind me that October is Popcorn Month. And mostly how she thinks whatever I do is awesome. When I accidentally put on mismatched socks, she calls it cool and artsy. She begs to see more of my goofy doodles. And she's really happy that I discovered I like debate.

Lunch is about a hundred times easier. Seriously. I don't have to feel so guilty every time I laugh at one of Jacob's jokes, or when I sneak a glance at him across the table. I can completely be me—no more mixed signals.

A few days later, during Social Studies, Ms. Yoon says we will no longer be working in our same groups or with the same partners. She explains that we are going to be starting an Ancient Roman history unit and that starting next week, we will be working with all new groups.

So today is the last day I'll be sitting with Jacob with our desks pushed together. I can feel my shoulders slumping at the news. For the next fifteen minutes, Ms. Yoon wants partners to discuss and process how we feel our debates went. What we can improve and what we enjoyed about working together.

"I don't think we could improve anything," says Jacob. "Working with you was awesome." He gives me a high five.

"Thanks," I say, suddenly feeling bashful.

"You were very determined, especially during the rebuttal."

"Yeah." Part of me wants to explain why I was really so heated up, but another part of me knows it will be too awkward to go into all of the details.

"There's nothing to improve," says Jacob. "It's hard to add awesome on top of awesome."

"Yeah, but we won't be seeing each other so much anymore," I say, doodling in the corner of my notebook.

"Well, there's lunch. And we pass by each other in the hall sometimes."

"It's not the same," I blurt.

"Yeah, true."

And then I say the bravest thing I've maybe ever said. "You want to hang out sometime?"

He studies me and the seconds stretch between us.

"Yeah, that'd be great. How about this Friday after school? We could meet at the Friendly Bean."

Yes! Yes! Yes! I want to leap out of my chair and do some kind of victory dance. Instead, I breathe in and out slowly and try to contain my excitement. "Yeah, sure. That'd be awesome." Was I being too gushy?

But he doesn't take back the offer. "So, around five? I've got to walk my neighbor's dog. They're away on a trip."

"I love dogs. If I had my choice, Morty, our labradoodle, would have a brother or a sister. And Jana has a poodle. His name is Gus."

"I remember." He leans forward. "I saw him by the soccer fields last week, when you were running away from me."

I can feel my face flush.

"Sorry about that. It had nothing to do with you. It was a thing between Jana and me."

He waves his hand in front of his face. "It's all right. You don't need to explain. I think I understand. Maybe it had something to do with the reason you also ran away from me at the mall?"

"Yeah, something like that." My cheeks grow warmer. But he's smiling and I'm smiling, and the end of our partnership suddenly doesn't feel like such an end.

The rest of the week feels like one giant countdown to meet Jacob at the Friendly Bean.

The paranoid part of me worries that somehow it's not going to work out. Like his parents are suddenly going to make him transfer back to his private school. Or I'm going to get sick. Actually, that part isn't totally crazy—on Wednesday, Fiona came down with a stomach virus and was out of school for two days, but not before she coughed her germs all over everyone, including me, during Social Studies.

Then Friday afternoon is finally, *finally*, here!

I park my bike on the rack outside of the Friendly Bean and slide my phone out of my pocket. Outside, the sky is milky white. I wanted it to be sunny and perfect for this day. I'm three minutes early. What should I do? Hang out here and wait until exactly five o'clock? Or should I walk in right now? A couple of moms with their strollers brush past me and go inside. The door clicks into place behind them.

I take the plunge, open the door, and walk inside. Jacob is there already standing in the back of the line. He waggles his fingers at me. I waggle my fingers back.

I go and stand in line with him. My fingers brush so close to his they practically touch.

"So, what would you like?" he says.

"Do you really need to ask?"

Grinning, he shakes his head. "Not really. But I figured you'd want something to eat."

Before I can respond, he continues. "Like a pumpkin spice muffin!"

"Exactly what I was going to say."

"I must be a mind reader, then. Because I have a feeling you'd also like a pumpkin spice frappé."

Some South American flute music wafts through

the coffee shop. The happy lilt matches my mood. I spot Elvie working behind the counter.

She smiles at me as she steams some milk.

Jacob and I chat about how Halloween should be an official town holiday and nobody should have to go to school that day. Soon it's our turn to order. Elvie nods and says hello, but doesn't do or say anything embarrassing. Like, "Why didn't you make your bed this morning?" or "You have something green stuck in your teeth." Nothing to make me feel like a little kid.

Jacob pays for me, which I totally don't expect. I pull some bills out of my wallet to pay him back, but he shakes his head. "Get it next time. This is on me."

Next time? I like the sound of that. My eyes graze the menu. "My sister gave us the muffin and brownie for half off, which is the employee discount."

"That's awesome," Jacob says, grinning.

"It's good to know people in high places." I poke his side with my elbow.

"I'll have to tell my brother to start working at Ben & Jerry's, then," he says. We find a small round table in the front of the store. I'm about to sit down when Jacob steps behind me.

"This might be on me"—he points at my cup of pumpkin spice—"but this is on you!" Then Jacob stuffs a bunch of ice cubes down the back of my shirt!

"Ahh!" I yelp, and wiggle and hop around until the cubes plink down onto the floor. I crouch to pick them up.

"Don't worry, it's just a couple of pieces," Jacob says.

"Oh, I'm not worrying!" I grab the ice cubes and lob them back at him.

He dodges, and the ice cubes land on the chair beside him. "Goalie training." Then his grin grows bigger. "Sorry, but I just had to do that. Stuff the ice down the back of your shirt, that is." He sits down.

"Thanks a lot," I say, but I'm not upset at all.

I sit across from him. We both study our drinks.

"It's nice here," he says.

"Yeah. It really is." I glance up and smile.

He reaches across the table and takes my hand.

We're actually holding hands. We're actually holding hands!

His skin is warm. "I also had to do that," he says.

Our eyes meet, and I notice for the first time that his reddish-brown hair is the exact color of pumpkin spice.

Yeah, pumpkin spice really is my favorite. And that's no secret.

About the Author

Hillary Homzie is the author of the tween novels *Queen of Likes*, *The Hot List*, and *Things Are Gonna Get Ugly*, as well as the comedic chapter book series Alien Clones From Outer Space. During the summers, Hillary teaches in the graduate program in children's writing at Hollins University. A former sketch comedy performer in New York City, Hillary currently lives with her family in Northern California.